Curse Of Blood Lagoon

Author:
Casey Christofferson

Editor:
Jeff Harkness

Swords & Wizardry Edition Conversion:
Jeff Harkness

Art Director:
Casey Christofferson

Interior Art:
Adrian Landeros and Santa Norvaisaite

Cover Art:
Adrian Landeros

Online Platforms Coordinator:
Sean King

Fantasy Grounds Conversion:
Michael G. Potter

Cartography:
Robert Altbauer

Layout:
Suzy Moseby

Cover Design:
Casey Christofferson

Necromancer Games
ISBN:978-1-6656-0185-6
SW PoD

TABLE OF CONTENTS

CURSE OF BLOOD LAGOON

BY CASEY CHRISTOFFERSON

A SWORDS & WIZARDRY ADVENTURE FOR 4–6 CHARACTERS OF LEVELS 4–5

Curse of Blood Lagoon is a **Swords & Wizardry** adventure for 4–6 characters of levels 4–5. The adventure is equal parts exploration of new locations and battle against supernatural foes. There are some puzzles to solve and traps to disarm, as well as an opportunity to save the Lost Lands from an insidious threat.

ADVENTURE BACKGROUND

On the isle known as Sea God's Lament, Lord Vayne Stanwyck and his private army settled on the shores of the interior island lagoon. Taking advantage of the tropical conditions, he raised crops for trade while kidnapping and forcing local islanders to work for his benefit. His operation remained successful for decades, though the islanders frequently rebelled against him and fought a lasting insurrection against his personal army. Before too long, his lucrative holdings gained the attention of the Brotherhood of Skulls.

The pirate confederation saw Lord Stanwyck as an easy mark and entered the lagoon with a trio of ships and quickly forced Vayne to surrender. Red-Handed Jaquez summarily put Stanwyck's men-at-arms to the sword. The blood spilled by the pirates on the shore of the harbor that day soaked the waters red, and they christened their new hideout the Blood Lagoon.

The pirates ruled in relative ease as the existing exporting operation served as a legitimate business front for their true nature. That is, until Merevok came to the Blood Lagoon like a thief in the night.

The ruthless magic-user with a benighted past brought with him the writings found on the *scale of Dagon*, a foul relic crafted from one of the deep one's own horrid scales. Through blood rituals, Merevok turned the pirates to the worship of Dagon, and even now sets out to unleash the curse of the Watery One upon the coastal lands! (See the **Curse of Dagon** sidebar for more on the curse.)

Through the course of the adventure, characters encounter *The Golden Snake*, a ship whose crew is under the sway of the curse of Dagon. Clues aboard the ship reveal the location of the Blood Lagoon on the Isle of the Sea God's Lament. Characters must then set forth in search of the Blood Lagoon to discover the source of the curse and stop it before Dagon's slithering horror engulfs their world.

CURSE OF DAGON

The rift created by the *scale of Dagon* brought out a host of semi-substantial demonic nematodes that attached themselves to the pirates who swore oaths to Dagon, filling their throats and occupying their bellies and lungs. The abyssal creatures slowly ravage their bodies so that when the beings are slain, they rise as a zombie possessed by the hive mind of the abyssal parasites that fill their flesh.

Any being who willingly drinks the waters polluted by the *scale of Dagon*, who submerge themselves in the corrupt waters, or who are bitten by an afflicted being must make a saving throw or become infected themselves. Those who fail their saving throw are filled with visions of chaos, madness, and the crushing waters of the abyssal deep. They are filled with a ravenous hunger to infect others with the curse as the nematodes replicate within their gullet. Cursed individuals talk with a gurgling noise and are absolutely fearless for their own safety.

Infected creatures are immune to *charm*, *sleep*, and *fear* effects. They gain +2 to attacks while alive (but they lose this bonus once they die and rise as zombies). They also receive a bite attack that does 1d2 points of damage and can infect the target with the demonic nematodes.

Beings infected with the curse of Dagon must make a saving throw each day or lose 1 point of constitution. When their constitution reaches zero, they die and rise in 1d4 rounds as a zombie that is also infected with the curse of Dagon.

Remove curse instantly destroys the demonic essence within the afflicted being's body, though they may be susceptible again if attacked or if they drink water infested with the nematodes. Casting *bless* or *protection from evil* on an infected creature allows them to make another save to vomit out the crawling nematodes. Forcing the victim to drink holy water also allows a new save. Alternatively, strong spirits such as rum, whisky, or brandy over which a *bless* spell has been cast instantly kills off the demonic nematodes and frees the victim of the curse.

Getting Started

Characters can begin the adventure in a variety of ways. A few suggestions are listed below to get the Referee started. Also supplied are the description of a small caravel and its crew who are at the characters' disposal for the duration of their adventure.

Holy Pilgrimage

The party's cleric or another holy person such as a paladin has been sent by their bishop to establish a temple in another country. On their journey, pirates infected with the curse of Dagon attack them. Documents aboard the ship point to the source of the curse being the Blood Lagoon.

Magical Anomaly

A leader of a wizards' guild — such as the Dominion Arcane — detected an unusual anomaly in the region of Sea God's Lament. The guild charters passage for a magic-user character and his allies to go and investigate the anomaly and report their findings back to the council.

By Writ of the King

A powerful noble hires the character to investigate raids on merchant shipping in the region of the Blood Lagoon. The characters are sent as a "bait fish" in order to incite an attack with the intent of taking a pirate leader prisoner in hopes of learning the location of the secret pirate base.

Assassination Game

Lord Stanwyck hasn't paid his creditors in months, and they hire the characters to assassinate Stanwyck and bring back a portion of his debt. In particular, they seek a magically locked coffer said to hold a small fortune in jewels. The characters are to be richly rewarded for their successful completion of the mission and for proof of Lord Stanwyck's termination.

Undoubtedly, other story hooks exist that work best for your campaign, and it is strongly encouraged that you use the one that best suits your needs.

Elmarran's Flute

This small, unarmed caravel is suited for sail with three lateen masts and has a capacity of 40 tons and a crew of 14 not counting the captain and the characters. A crew of nine can sail the ship successfully, however. If the characters do not have their own ship or some other means of conveyance, *Elmarran's Flute* serves as their transportation for the course of the adventure, or until they trade up to a different vessel should they manage to locate sufficient crew to man the sails. **Oldport Maggie**, an able dwarf captain who has plied the tradeways of the seas for the better part of 50 years, captains *Elmarran's Flute*.

Oldport Maggie, Female Dwarf Captain (Ftr3/Thf3): HP 16; **AC** 6[13]; **Atk** *+1 cutlass* (1d6+2); **Move** 9; **Save** 12; **AL** N; **CL/XP** 6/400; **Special:** +1 to hit and damage strength bonus, +2 save bonus vs. traps and magical devices, backstab (x2), darkvision (60ft), detect stonework, multiple attacks (3) vs. creatures with 1 or fewer HD, read languages, thieving skills.

Thieving Skills: Climb 87%, Tasks/Traps 35%, Hear 4 in 6, Hide 25%, Silent 35%, Locks 25%.

Equipment: *+1 leather armor*, *+1 cutlass*, *potion of healing* (x3), gold rope chain (200 gp), ruby-encrusted bracelet (500 gp), pearl earrings (250 gp), 1,500 gp.

Maggie is friendly to the characters after her own fashion; she is crusty, cantankerous, and does whatever it takes to protect her ship and the crew she loves. Maggie never willingly leads *Elmarran's Flute* into a danger that would cause hull damage to the boat.

Elmarran's Flute **Crew, Male or Female Humans (Ftr2) (14):** HP 16, 15x3, 14, 13x2, 11, 10x3, 9, 8x2; **AC** 7[12]; **Atk** cutlass (1d6), dagger (1d4), belaying pin (club) (1d4); **Move** 12; **Save** 13; **AL** N; **CL/XP** 2/30; **Special:** multiple attacks (2) vs. creatures with 1 or fewer HD.

Equipment: leather armor, cutlass, dagger, belaying pin (club), rum, tobacco, gold trinkets and pearls (20 gp total).

The crew of *Elmarran's Flute* fight for Oldport Maggie and to save their own lives if the ship is attacked. However, they are not mercenaries or hirelings at the characters' undisputed disposal. They cannot be called on as some invasion force, and are as likely to put the characters onto lifeboats and let them row to shore as they are to sail their ship up the Vayne River.

Attack of The Golden Snake

The adventure begins as the characters are sailing on their own ship or find themselves passengers on *Elmarran's Flute*. The characters are several days from the mainland and approaching an area of coastal islands known for piracy. The characters recently came into possession of a treasure map that would guide them to a larger land mass a month's journey from their place of departure.

Shortly after sundown, the crew of *The Golden Snake* attacks the characters' ship. Characters watching the waves have a 2-in-6 chance to notice the approach of the fast-moving vessel.

If the characters discover the silent approach of the enemy vessel, allow them to raise whatever alarm they find necessary to rouse the crew and prepare to repel boarders.

Ship-to-Ship Battle

If the characters notice the approach of the vessel sailing next to them in the darkness of night, allow them an additional action before combat commences. Such an action may include a free missile attack or an opportunity to rouse sleeping crewmembers. If the characters miss their opportunity to notice the maddened crew of *The Golden Snake*, the ship pulls alongside *Elmarran's Flute*, and its crew hurls grappling hooks that quickly lash the ships together. They attack by swarming over the side of *Elmarran's Flute*, rapidly attempting to grapple and subdue any opposing sailors so they can quickly be infected with the demonic curse.

The Referee may run the battle as he wishes, or he may assume the crew of *Elmarran's Flute* are overpowered by the crew of *The Golden Snake* at a rate of 2-to-1, leaving all remainders to battle the characters.

To simplify things, the crew of *Elmarran's Flute* occupy seven of the boarders, leaving the characters to manage Red-Handed Jaquez and nine other cursed pirates by themselves. For every two rounds the characters take against Jaquez's cursed crew, one crewmember of *Elmarran's Flute* succumbs to Dagon's curse, adding another opponent for the characters to face.

Build on the horror of the fact that as pirates "die" in battle, they rise again in 1d4 rounds as undead creatures, still bent on infecting their hosts with the demonic curse!

What's All This Nonsense About No Cannons?

Cannons and bombards have been in use in medieval combat for roughly the same equivalent time of human history as the development and use of plate armor. As the majority of fantasy RPGs take place in homogenized campaign worlds where Viking longships are as common a sight on the open seas as carracks or caravels invented some 300 years after the Viking era, it begs the question why fantasy RPG authors are reluctant to use equipment and materials that emerged during the eras they so lovingly reimagine. Historically speaking, cannons mounted aboard ships were first used in the battle of Arnemuiden in 1338. As the cannons developed, so did the armor, though largely for different reasons. Thus, in a world where dragons, fairies, and giants exist, where magic-users can call down bolts of lightning or wield balls of magical fire, why wouldn't there be cannons aboard ships? If, however, you happen to hold some sort of grudge against firearms or are still drinking that "magic powder" beverage that was sold to you in the 1980s, by all means substitute any reference to a sensible bombard mentioned in this adventure with a similarly sized, though vastly more ridiculous ballista.

The Golden Snake

The Golden Snake is a fast-moving caravel rigged for piracy. It carries no cargo, save a month's rations for the crew. It is outfitted with six six-pound guns. Though it can bring only three to bear per side, and has no forward firing ability. It has a crew of **16 pirates** infected with the demonic curse, which is driving them mad and causing them to fight beyond their own sense of safety while in combat.

Red-Handed Jaquez is the captain of *The Golden Snake*. A sharp-eyed corsair, Jaquez was already known for offering no quarter to his prey even before succumbing to the demonic curse.

The Golden Snake Crew

The crew of *The Golden Snake* is composed of hard-bitten pirates with years of experience at sail. The pirates are infected with the demonic curse of Dagon. They are immune to *fear*, *sleep*, and pain of any sort. When they die, they rise as zombies, meaning they must die twice in order to be destroyed!

***The Golden Snake* Pirates, Male or Female Human Sailors (Ftr3) (16):** HP 22, 20x2, 19, 18x3, 17, 15x2, 14x3, 13x2, 10; AC 7[12]; **Atk** cutlass (1d6), light crossbow (1d4+1) or bite (1d2 + infection); **Move** 12; **Save** 12; **AL** C; **CL/XP** 3/60; **Special:** +2 to hit, infection (Dagon's curse, save avoids), multiple attacks (3) vs. creatures with 1 or fewer HD.

Equipment: leather armor, cutlass, light crossbow and 10 bolts, grappling hook, 50 feet rope, and rum, tobacco, gold trinkets and pearls (200 gp total).

Note: The pirates are infected with the demonic plague and are immune to *fear*, *sleep*, and *charm person*. The pirates rise as **zombies** 1d4 rounds after death.

Zombie Pirates (varies): HD 2; AC 8[11]; **Atk** cutlass (1d6) or bite (1d2 + infection); **Move** 6; **Save** 16; **AL** N; **CL/XP** 2/30; **Special:** immune to *sleep* and *charm*, infection (Dagon's curse, save avoids).

Captain Red-Handed Jaquez, Male Human Captain (Asn7): HP 32; AC 5[14]; **Atk** *+1 cutlass* (1d6+1 + 1d6 poison) or *+1 light crossbow* (1d4+2 + 1d6 poison); **Move** 12; **Save** 8 (+1, ring); **AL** C; **CL/XP** 7/600; **Special:** +2 to hit, backstab (x3), disguise, read languages, thieving skills.

Thieving Skills: Climb 89%, Tasks/Traps 35%, Hear 4 in 6, Hide 30%, Silent 40%, Locks 30%.

Equipment: *+1 leather armor*, *+1 cutlass*, *+1 light crossbow* with 20 bolts, *potion of healing* (x2), *ring of protection +1*, 2 vials of poison (1d6 damage, save resists), spyglass, 1500gp.

Note: Jaquez is infected with Dagon's curse. He is immune to *fear*, *sleep*, and *charm person*. He rises as a **brine zombie** 1d4 rounds after death.

Brine Zombie Jaquez: HD 4; HP 27; AC 5[14]; **Atk** *+1 cutlass* (1d6+1 + 1d6 poison) or bite (1d2 + infection); **Move** 12 (swim 12); **Save** 12 (+1, ring); **AL** C; **CL/XP** 4/120; **Special:** immune to *sleep* and *charm*, infection (Dagon's curse, save avoids), resistance to fire (50%), *ring of protection +1*. (***The Tome of Horrors Complete*** 614)

Equipment: *+1 leather armor*, *+1 cutlass*, *ring of protection +1*. Among Jaquez's charts is a map to Sea God's Lament, a rough map of the Blood Lagoon and documents listing 1,000 pounds of gold, 1,000 pounds of silver, and the word "Cho Sun's Rotten Blood" written in between a pair of towers drawn at the entrance to the lagoon.

SEA GOD'S LAMENT
1 Square - 1/2 Mile
8
7
6
5
2
3
4
N
x
1
x - Shipwreck

It is of course possible that the characters refuse to heed the call of adventure once they discover evidence of a horrible magical plague and the possibility of it infesting their home country. Should they decide to do what 90% of shipboard adventurers do and ignore the adventure completely, it is time for the Referee to break out "ye olde squall" and shipwreck the characters on the shores of Sea God's Lament, not so far from **Location 3: Shipwreck Isle** on the **Island Map.**

Roll lots of dice to add to the excitement of surviving the storm, but ensure that the characters all find themselves washed ashore with their basic gear intact. The storm damages the ship, requiring several days of repairs before it is seaworthy. Oldport Maggie and the crew engage in these repairs immediately.

Note: The storm option should be used only if players lose their minds and decide to skip searching for the island altogether. You know, like they do.

Look, an Island!

Another option for getting the characters into the Blood Lagoon is for them to "accidentally" encounter the Isle of the Sea God's Lament. In this encounter, the winds have blown them in a northerly direction. They spot the island easily and note its central mountain and the wide mouth of the Vayne River.

A Destination for Fun and Adventure! The Isle of the Sea God's Lament

The following locations use the Island Map: Sea God's Lament

The Isle of the Sea God's Lament: This outer coastal isle known as Sea God's Lament is a 400-square-mile island situated a mere 100 miles off the continental shores. The island has exported crops and served as a smugglers' base, and most recently was claimed as a pirate base.

Sea God's Lament Random Encounters

1d12	Vayne River Encounter
1	1d4 bull sharks
2	1d6 giant crayfish
3	Giant crocodile
4	2d4 lacedons
5	1d2 trolls
6	Pirate skiff
7–12	No encounter

Giant Crocodile: This encounter is with a **giant crocodile**. It attacks anything the size of a skiff or smaller, looking to capsize the vessel and drown anyone thrown into the water for later consumption.
Giant Crocodile: HD 6; AC 3[16]; Atk bite (3d6), tail (1d6); Move 9 (swim 12); Save 11; AL N; CL/XP 6/400; Special: none. (*Monstrosities* 78)
Bull Sharks: This is an encounter with **1d4 seven-foot-long bull sharks.** They ignore ships but attack anyone wading in shallow water.
Medium Shark (1d4): HD 5; AC 6[13]; Atk bite (1d6+2); Move 0 (swim 24); Save 12; AL N; CL/XP 5/240; Special: feeding frenzy (1-in-6 chance of targeting another shark). (*Monstrosities* 420)
Giant Crayfish: This encounter is with **1d6 giant crawfish.** These crustaceans see the characters as nice soft grubs and attack.
Giant Crayfish (1d6): HD 4; AC 4[15]; Atk 2 claws (1d6); Move 9 (swim 15); Save 13; AL N; CL/XP 4/120; Special: surprise (1–2 on 1d6). (*Monstrosities* 78)
Lacedons: These submerged ghouls are the remains of pirates who died while infected with Dagon's curse. The **2d4 lacedons** attack from surprise, either clambering aboard ship or dragging waders and swimmers underwater.

Lacedons (Ghouls) (2d4): HD 2; AC 6[13]; Atk 2 claws (1d3 + paralysis), bite (1d4 + infection); Move 9 (swim 12); Save 16; AL C; CL/XP 3/60; Special: immunities (*charm*, *sleep*), infection (Dagon's curse, save avoids), paralyzing touch (3d6 turns, save avoids).
Pirate Skiff: This small seagoing coastal skiff holds **8 pirates** infected with Dagon's curse. The pirates are unconcerned for their own safety and fight to the death — only to rise again as animated fiends.
Pirates, Male or Female Human Sailors (Ftr1) (8): HP 1d8; AC 7[12]; Atk cutlass (1d6) or bite (1d2 + infection); Move 12; Save 14; AL C; CL/XP 1/15; Special: +2 to hit.
Equipment: leather armor, cutlass, rum, tobacco, and gold trinkets (3gp total).
Note: The pirates are infected with the demonic plague and are immune to *fear*, *sleep*, and *charm person*. The pirates rise as **zombies** 1d4 rounds after death.
Zombie Pirates (8): HD 2; AC 8[11]; Atk cutlass (1d6) or bite (1d2 + infection); Move 6; Save 16; AL N; CL/XP 2/30; Special: immune to *sleep* and *charm*, infection (Dagon's curse, save avoids).
Troll: This encounter is with **1d2 trolls.**
Trolls (1d2): HD 6+3; AC 4[15]; Atk 2 claws (1d4), bite (1d8); Move 12; Save 11; AL C; CL/XP 8/800; Special: regenerate (3hp/round).

1. Vayne River

The mouth of the Vayne River as it opens to the Blood Lagoon is deep enough to handle the keel of the most common ships of the regional seas. The river's current is fairly easygoing as well. The water here is warm and teems with crayfish, freshwater oysters, and large catfish, as well as some bull sharks, and native crocodiles of both the small and giant varieties.

The Vayne River is a twisting freshwater river that runs upland for 20 miles, growing increasingly shallower with every mile, until it becomes impassible by ship just south of the island's highland region.

2. East Isle

The East Isle is a small island formed by the tributaries of the Vayne River on the eastern side of the great isle. This island is heavily wooded with bald cypress near the riverside and old oak deeper inland. Crocodiles, snakes, and swarms of biting insects inhabit East Isle.

1d12	Encounter
1	1d4+2 islanders
2	1d6 pirate ghouls
3	Giant crocodile
4	Giant constrictor snake
5	Insect swarm
7	Strangle weed
8	1d4 wild boars
9–12	No encounter

Crocodile: This encounter is with a **giant crocodile**. It attacks anything the size of a skiff or smaller, looking to capsize the vessel and drown anyone thrown into the water for later consumption.
Giant Crocodile: HD 6; AC 3[16]; Atk bite (3d6), tail (1d6); Move 9 (swim 12); Save 11; AL N; CL/XP 6/400; Special: none. (*Monstrosities* 78)
Giant Constrictor Snake: This **constrictor snake** seeks to coil around its prey, crushing it, before dragging it to a nearby lair to devour. The attack is stealthy and quick.
Giant Constrictor: HD 6; AC 5[14]; Atk bite (1d3), constrict (2d4); Move 10; Save 11; AL N; CL/XP 7/600; Special: constrict (automatic damage after hit, 1-in-6 chance to pin prey's arm). (*Monstrosities* 440)
Insect Swarm: A large **swarm of insects** descends on the party, crawling under armor and inside clothes, ferociously stinging and biting.
Islander: This is an encounter with **1d4 + 2 islanders.** These barbarians are armed with cutlasses taken from pirates, spears, and shortbows. They wear hide armor.

Islanders, Male or Female Humans (Ftr2) (1d4+2): HD 2d8; **AC** 7[12]; **Atk** cutlass (1d6), spear (1d6) or shortbow x2 (1d6); **Move** 12; **Save** 13; **AL** C; **CL/XP** 2/30; **Special:** multiple attacks (2) vs. creatures with 1 or fewer HD, rage (+1 to hit and damage, 4 rounds/day).

Equipment: leather armor, cutlass, 5 spears, shortbow with 10 arrows.

Pirate Ghouls: These **1d6 ghouls**, dressed in the trappings of the pirates of the Blood Lagoon, wander the island in search of rotted flesh to eat. They are infected with Dagon's curse.

Pirate Ghouls (1d6): HD 2; **AC** 6[13]; **Atk** 2 claws (1d3 + paralysis), bite (1d4 + infection); **Move** 9; **Save** 16; **AL** C; **CL/XP** 3/60; **Special:** immunities (*charm*, *sleep*), infection (Dagon's curse, save avoids), paralyzing touch (3d6 turns, save avoids).

Note: The ghouls are infected with Dagon's curse. They rise as **zombies** 1d4 rounds after death.

Zombies (varies): HD 2; **AC** 8[11]; **Atk** cutlass (1d6) or bite (1d2 + infection); **Move** 6; **Save** 16; **AL** N; **CL/XP** 2/30; **Special:** immune to *sleep* and *charm*, infection (Dagon's curse, save avoids).

Strangle Weed: This encounter is with a patch of **strangle weed**, which grows profusely on the island.

Strangle Weed: HD 4; **AC** 5[14]; **Atk** slam (1d6); **Move** 3; **Save** 13; **AL** N; **CL/XP** 5/240; **Special:** camouflage, constriction (save or be held, automatic 1d6 points of damage per round), resist fire (50%), surprise (1–4 on 1d6). (***The Tome of Horrors Complete*** 523)

Wild Boar: This is an encounter with **1d4 regular wild boars**.

Wild Boars (1d4): HD 3+3; **AC** 7[12]; **Atk** gore (3d4); **Move** 15; **Save** 14; **AL** N; **CL/XP** 4/120; **Special:** continue attacks two rounds after death. (***Monstrosities*** 48)

3. Shipwreck Isle

Named for a shipwrecked caravel that lies broken in two along its southern shore, Shipwreck Isle serves as a lookout point for Merevok's demon-haunted pirates. The island is bordered by the sea, the wide mouth of the Vayne River, and one of its lesser tributaries.

A. Lookout

Hidden among the treetops are a pair of afflicted pirates who scan the sea for incoming sails and passing ships. If they see any prey, they signal one of the ships anchored in the lagoon, and a crew is raised to set out to attack. The lookouts signal the lagoon's tower by way of hand mirrors. The lookouts do not stay to fight anyone who decides to disembark and investigate the shipwreck. Rather, they let the traps and ghouls left behind at the shipwreck do their dirty work for them.

B. The Shipwreck

The Blue Crab was a merchant caravel captured by pirates and used to transport loot until it got caught upon the reefs during bad weather several years ago. The ship split in two and washed ashore on the island known on some maps as South Isle. Although some of its crew survived, Lord Stanwyck eventually captured the crew and put them to work upon his estate. Since the coming of Merevok, the ship has been ghoulishly adorned (literally) with the corpses of trespassers and pirates who disappointed the demonologist in his pursuits. The rotting corpses of sailors not possessed by Dagon have had their throats slit and their bodies nailed to the rotting timbers of the remains of *The Blue Crab*. Traps have been lain to ensnare the curious, and **2d6 ghouls** roam the timbers, waiting to murder explorers so that they may feast on their sunbaked corpses.

Ghouls (2d6): HD 2; **AC** 6[13]; **Atk** 2 claws (1d3 + paralysis), bite (1d4); **Move** 9; **Save** 16; **AL** C; **CL/XP** 3/60; **Special:** immunities (*charm*, *sleep*), paralyzing touch (3d6 turns, save avoids).

1d4	Trap Type
1	**Deadfall Trap:** Planking has been set up to cause a section of the ship's timbers to fall onto characters tripping the trap and anyone within a five-foot-by-10-foot area. The trap does 2d6 points of damage (save for half).
2	**Ballista (or Cannon) Trap:** Ballista (or cannon) on the deck of the ship are strung with lengths of chain and detonate when the tripwire is set, firing at anyone in a 10-foot-by-10-foot area. The trap deals 3d6 points of damage (save for half).
3	**Pit Trap:** This is a common pit trap dug near the shipwreck, and covered with debris. The trap is 10 feet deep and filled with five feet of brackish water, so there is no damage from the fall. A **ghast** that slunk into the water hungrily waits for prey. **Ghast:** HD 4; HP 26; AC 4[15]; Atk 2 claws (1d3), bite (1d6); **Move** 15; **Save** 13; **AL** C; **CL/XP** 5/240; **Special:** paralyzing touch (3d6 turns, save avoids), stench (10ft, save or suffer −2 to-hit penalty). (*Monstrosities* 189)
4	**Cargo Net Trap:** This trap springs a large cargo net over a 10-foot-by-20-foot area that affects targets equivalent to a *web* spell. Fire does not instantly burn the net due to the humidity of the island. Any surviving ghouls not caught up in the net as well attack entangled characters.

4. Western Tributaries

These narrow channels are too shallow for the passage of any full-sized ship, though a flatboat or canoe would be able to navigate their murky backwaters with ease. The tributaries are home to crocodiles and a den of trolls who dwell in mud-and-wattle huts near the center of the large island.

1d12	Encounter
1	1d4 + 1 trolls (troll nest)
2	1d4 crocodiles
3	Giant venomous snake (1) or 50% chance of "snake ball" (2d4 giant snakes)
4	2d4 giant frogs
5	Strangle weed
6	1d4 wild boars
7–12	No encounter

Crocodiles: This encounter is with **1d4 crocodiles**.
Crocodiles (1d4): HD 3; AC 4[15]; Atk bite (1d6); Move 9 (swim 12); Save 14; AL N; CL/XP 3/60; Special: none. (*Monstrosities* 77)
Giant Frogs: These toothed frogs are large enough to devour a halfling or other small-sized character in one bite (natural roll of 20 to hit).
Giant Frog (medium) (2d4): HD 2; AC 7[12]; Atk bite (1d6); Move 3 (or 100ft leap); Save 16; AL N; CL/XP 2/30; Special: leap. (*Monstrosities* 179)
Giant Venomous Snake: This giant venomous snake attacks from surprise, attempting to poison and drag away its prey to eat at its leisure. The snake grabs its victim and moves away from any others at its maximum rate of speed, moving toward water or thick underbrush. There is a 50% chance that the characters instead encounter a "snake ball," a knot of **2d4 giant snakes** swarming in a roughly spherical form.
Giant Viper: HD 4; AC 5[14]; Atk bite (1d3 + poison); Move 12; Save 13; AL N; CL/XP 6/400; Special: lethal poison (save or die). (*Monstrosities* 440)
Strangle Weed: This encounter is with a patch of **strangle weed**, which grows profusely on the island.
Strangle Weed: HD 4; AC 5[14]; Atk slam (1d6); Move 3; Save 13; AL N; CL/XP 5/240; Special: camouflage, constriction (save or be held, automatic 1d6 points of damage per round), resist fire (50%), surprise (1–4 on 1d6). (*The Tome of Horrors Complete* 523)

The Troll Nest: Hidden beneath the roots of a giant cypress tree is the troll nest. These **1d4 + 1 trolls** avoid the pirates who burned some of their ilk when they went to parley with the pirates after the pirates killed Lord Stanwyck and took over his operation. The trolls make use of the waters around their nest to thwart attempts to burn them out. The water is at least waist deep to man-sized explorers, and reduces movement by half.
Trolls (1d4 + 1): HD 6+3; AC 4[15]; Atk 2 claws (1d4), bite (1d8); Move 12; Save 11; AL C; CL/XP 8/800; Special: regenerate (3hp/round).
Treasure: The trolls have accumulated 300 gp, a gallon of overproof rum, a jewel-handled rapier worth 200 gp, and the green skins of three giant wild boars that, if properly tanned, would net about 10 gp each.
Wild Boar: This is an encounter with **1d4 regular wild boars**.
Wild Boars (1d4): HD 3+3; AC 7[12]; Atk gore (3d4); Move 15; Save 14; AL N; CL/XP 4/120; Special: continue attacks two rounds after death. (*Monstrosities* 48)

5. Sessenni's Island

This heavily forested island is named after Sessenni, a holy woman of the original inhabitants of the island who Lord Stanwyck captured when he conquered the area. Sessenni's spirit is said to dwell here, so the pirates avoid the island. The island is known for being quiet, as not even a bird lands among the boughs of its trees.

Sessenni is a **banshee** trapped upon the island by the flowing waters of the Vayne River. She appears only after dark. Haunting the island with her are Lord Stanwyck's children (now **2 skull children**), whom Sessenni's spirit coaxed to the island with her song and killed. She now "raises" the children herself as a cruel form of retribution for the "loss" of her own child. Hunters forced her to drop her babe into the waters of the river and then tortured her to death at the behest of Lord Stanwyck's wife.
Sessenni (Banshee): HD 7; HP 49; AC 0[19]; Atk claw (1d8); **Move** 12 (fly); **Save** 9; **AL** C; **CL/XP** 11/1700; **Special:** +1 magical or silver weapon to hit, immune to enchantments, magic resistance (49%), shriek of death (1/day, save or die in 2d6 rounds). (*Monstrosities* 30)
Vayne III and Georgia (Skull Children): HD 5; HP 36, 30; AC 4 [15]; Atk 2 claws (1d4 + energy drain), bite (1d6 + weakness); **Move** 9; **Save** 12; **AL** C; **CL/ XP** 10/1400; **Special:** create spawn (juveniles rise in 24 hours as skull child), energy drain (1 level if both claws hit in the same round), masquerade (*detect evil* fails between dawn and dusk), powerless in sunlight, terrifying gaze (save or unable to act for 1d4 rounds), weakness (−2 to hit and damage, save avoids). (*Tome of Horrors 4* 196)

Vayne III and Georgia were raised in a climate of cruelty. They possessed an abject lack of moral compass in life, often observing their father and his overseer's cruelty to the native islander population. The skull children's tactics involve calling others to Sessenni's lair near the center of the island with cries of help before turning on survivors of Sessenni's groaning call. Other tactics involve appearing in the forest, then slipping deep among the trees if followed. They try to separate opponents and turn their terrors upon the survivors.

Treasure: Vayne and Georgia possess lockets featuring pictures of Lord Stanwyck and Lady Marie as they appeared in life. The lockets are gold and worth 50 gp each. Sessenni's collapsed cabin in the center of the island contains a cache of scrolls, including scrolls of *protection from good, cause serious wounds, neutralize poison, restoration*, and two scrolls of *remove curse*.

6. Eastern Pine Islands

These scrub pines grow on the eastern tributaries of the Vayne River. The pirates avoid the pine islands, as they are infested with nests of **stirges**. There is a 20% chance every 10 minutes spent on the pine islands of encountering a stirge nest. The stirges swarm victims once they smell hot blood.
Stirge Nest (2d10 stirges): HD 1+1; AC 7[12]; Atk proboscis (1d3); **Move** 3 (fly 18); **Save** 17; **AL** N; **CL/XP** 2/30; **Special:** +2 to hit bonus, blood drain (1d4).
Stirge: HD 1+1; AC 7[12]; Atk proboscis (1d3); **Move** 3 (fly 18); **Save** 17; **AL** N; **CL/XP** 2/30; **Special:** +2 to-hit bonus, blood drain (1d4).

7. Interior Island Forest

This dense rainforest is home to a variety of tropical beasts. Hiding here are survivors of Sessenni's people who learned to stay clear of the pirates who seek only to capture them and use them as forced labor. The islanders have not gained sufficient strength to create any challenge to the pirate settlement at the Blood Lagoon. With the arrival of Merevok, they are even more reluctant to face the horrors that the mad wizard has unleashed upon the island.

1d6	Encounter
1	2d4 escaped captives
2	1d6 pirate ghouls
3	Strangle weed
4	Islander war band (1d4 + 2 barbarians)
5	1d4 wild boars
6	Crazy fruit grove

Crazy Fruit Grove: The characters stumble into a grove of crazy fruit. There is a 50% chance of **1d4 + 2 pirates** sitting in the grove, whacked out of their minds on the fruit. They see the characters and assume that they are demons. They suffer −2 to hit but deal +2 damage on a successful hit. There are 2d12 ripe crazy fruit growing in the trees of the grove, and countless other unripened fruits.

Pirates, Male or Female Human Sailors (Ftr1) (1d4 + 2): HP 1d8; AC 7[12]; Atk cutlass (1d6+2) or bite (1d2 + infection); **Move** 12; **Save** 14; **AL** C; **CL/XP** 1/15; **Special:** crazy fruit influence (−2 to hit, +2 damage), infection (Dagon's curse, save avoids).

Equipment: leather armor, cutlass, rum, tobacco, and gold trinkets (3 gp total).

Note: The pirates are infected with the demonic plague and are immune to *fear*, *sleep*, and *charm person*. The pirates rise as **zombies** 1d4 rounds after death. They are out of their minds on crazy fruit.

Zombie Pirates (varies): HD 2; **AC** 8[11]; **Atk** cutlass (1d6) or bite (1d2 + infection); **Move** 6; **Save** 16; **AL** N; **CL/XP** 2/30; **Special:** immune to *sleep* and *charm*, infection (Dagon's curse, save avoids).

Escaped Captives: These former captives hide in the forest to avoid being recaptured by pirates or being infected by the curse of Dagon. The captives are armed with knives taken from the supply locker at Lord Stanwyck's estate.

Escaped Captives, Male or Female Humans (2d4): HD 1d6; **AC** 7[12]; **Atk** cane knife (1d4); **Move** 12; **Save** 18; **AL** C; **CL/XP** B/10; **Special:** none.

Equipment: cane knife.

Islander War Band: This is an encounter with **1d4 + 2 islander barbarians**. They may not necessarily attack the characters, but they let it be known that the characters are not welcome in their part of the island. The war band is armed with spears and cutlasses, and wear hide armor.

Islanders, Male or Female Humans (Ftr2) (1d4 + 2): HD 2d8; **AC** 7[12]; **Atk** cutlass (1d6), spear (1d6) or shortbow x2 (1d6); **Move** 12; **Save** 13; **AL** C; **CL/XP** 2/30; **Special:** multiple attacks (2) vs. creatures with 1 or fewer HD, rage (+1 to hit and damage, 4 rounds/day).

Equipment: leather armor, cutlass, 5 spears, shortbow with 10 arrows.

Pirate Ghouls: These **1d6 ghouls**, dressed in the trappings of the pirates of the Blood Lagoon, wander the island in search of rotted flesh to eat. They are infected with Dagon's curse.

Pirate Ghouls (1d6): HD 2; **AC** 6[13]; **Atk** 2 claws (1d3 + paralysis), bite (1d4 + infection); **Move** 9; **Save** 16; **AL** C; **CL/XP** 3/60; **Special:** immunities (*charm*, *sleep*), infection (Dagon's curse, save avoids), paralyzing touch (3d6 turns, save avoids).

Note: The ghouls are infected with Dagon's curse. They rise as **zombies** 1d4 rounds after death.

Zombies (varies): HD 2; **AC** 8[11]; **Atk** cutlass (1d6) or bite (1d2 + infection); **Move** 6; **Save** 16; **AL** N; **CL/XP** 2/30; **Special:** immune to *sleep* and *charm*, infection (Dagon's curse, save avoids).

Strangle Weed: This encounter is with a patch of **strangle weed**, which grows profusely on the island.

Strangle Weed: HD 4; **AC** 5[14]; **Atk** slam (1d6); **Move** 3; **Save** 13; **AL** N; **CL/XP** 5/240; **Special:** camouflage, constriction (save or be held, automatic 1d6 points of damage per round), resist fire (50%), surprise (1–4 on 1d6). (**The Tome of Horrors Complete** 523)

Wild Boar: This is an encounter with **1d4 regular wild boars**.

Wild Boars (1d4): HD 3+3; **AC** 7[12]; **Atk** gore (3d4); **Move** 15; **Save** 14; **AL** N; **CL/XP** 4/120; **Special:** continue attacks two rounds after death. (**Monstrosities** 48)

Forest Settlement

Hidden in the interior forest is a settlement of the island's refugees. This mixture of escaped captives and original island inhabitants has dwindled to fewer than 30 adult individuals, 10 elderly, and 10 children. **Greamoa**, an elder and druid who was born on the island, leads them. They occasionally rescue captives from the pirates and once waged a guerrilla war on Lord Stanwyck. When the pirates took over, they freed the locals and generally ignored the natives as they shifted their own operations to detaining those unfortunate souls they captured on the high seas. Greamoa's people have been spared the depredations of Merevok's crusade. Among the islanders are **30 escaped captives** who made their way into the interior as the pirates attacked one another. Many were descendants of Greamoa's folk in the first place.

Islanders, Male or Female Humans (Ftr1) (30): HD 1d8; **AC** 7[12]; **Atk** club (1d4), spear (1d6); **Move** 12; **Save** 14; **AL** C; **CL/XP** 1/15; **Special:** rage (+1 to hit and damage, 2 rounds/day).

Equipment: leather armor, club, 5 spears.

Escaped Captives, Male or Female Humans (30): HD 1d6; **AC** 7[12]; **Atk** cane knife (1d4); **Move** 12; **Save** 18; **AL** C; **CL/XP** B/10; **Special:** none.

Equipment: cane knife.

Greamoa, Female Human Elder (Drd6): HP 29; **AC** 4[15]; **Atk** *+1 scimitar* (1d6+1), spear (1d6); **Move** 9; **Save** 10; **AL** N; **CL/XP** 6/400; **Special:** +2 save vs. fire, shape change, immune to fey charms, spells (4/2/2/1).

Spells: 1st—*detect magic, detect snares and pits, locate animals, purify water*; 2nd—*cure light wounds, obscuring mist*; 3rd—*call lightning, cure disease*; 4th—*cure serious wounds*.

Equipment: *+1 scimitar*, 5 spears, *bracers of defense AC 4[15]*.

What the Refugees May Share

Some of those who escaped the pirates joined Merevok and now guard him as if he were a god atop the mountain in the center of the island. It is unknown if they succumbed to the curse or if they serve him willingly, though it is believed they have eaten the "crazy fruit" that grows in the island's interior forest.

Crazy Fruit

Crazy fruit is a wild fruit that grows on some trees in the forest. It is the size of a lumpy green and pink grapefruit. The fruit itself is harmless and nourishing. The birds, beasts, and natives of the island have eaten it for untold centuries.

The fruits' seeds, however, have an intoxicating effect on whoever chews them, causing mild hallucinations, a feeling of euphoria, fearlessness, and occasionally explosive diarrhea, or death. The islanders use a distillate of the seeds in their celebrations of adulthood, with stronger admixtures saved for their holy men and seers.

Characters eating the seeds must make a saving throw. If the save fails, the character is afflicted with instantaneous diarrhea and hallucinations that make the character see demons and other unholy apparitions for 1d2 hours. Rolling a 1 on the save attempt means the character dies from overheating and dehydration in 1d2 hours unless a *cure disease* spell is cast on the character.

---

8. The Blood Lagoon

The next section details the environs around the Blood Lagoon.

The Blood Lagoon

Characters have a variety of approaches to enter the Blood Lagoon. They could sail up the Vayne River itself and enter the mouth of the lagoon directly. Other means include navigating a skiff up the tributaries and hacking through the forest south of Lord Stanwyck's estate, or they may exit the river north of the lagoon and cross through the inland forests to the north.

1. Vayne River

The Vayne River is described elsewhere. At this point in the river, the current is slow and languid, and the water is 50 feet deep, affording plenty of room for a standard-sized sailing vessel to navigate the waters.

2. The Towers and Chain

The river entrance to the lagoon is flanked on both sides by two 20-foot-tall wooden watchtowers and a palisade wall. The towers are covered in the dried green skins of animals, crudely nailed to the walls, and are soaked with water to protect against fire attacks if ships are sighted entering the Vayne River.

A great chain lies beneath the water between the two watchtowers. The pirates operate a crank and pulley mechanism to pull the chain up from the water to block any ships entering the Blood Lagoon. Ships sailing against the chain suffer hull damage. The amount and severity of this damage is at the discretion of the Referee.

Characters attempting to sail directly past the watchtowers may do so, but an alarm is raised that sends pursuit skiffs filled with cursed pirates upriver after them unless they make their attempt after dark while hugging the eastern banks of the river.

Wooden Watchtowers

Manning each watchtower are **6 pirates** infected by the demonic plague. The pirates are armed with heavy crossbows and cutlasses. Normally, they fire in volleys of three per tower while their comrades reload. Crazed with the demonic plague, however, the pirates make every attempt to board ships trapped in the harbor by the chain. They hurl grapples into the rigging of invading ships and swing down from the tower onto the deck of an invading ship.

Pirates, Male or Female Human Sailors (Ftr1) (12 total, 6 per tower): HP 8x2, 7x2, 6x6, 5x2; AC 7[12]; Atk cutlass (1d6), heavy crossbow (1d6+1) or bite (1d2 + infection); **Move** 12; **Save** 14; **AL** C; **CL/XP** 1/15; **Special:** +2 to hit, infection (Dagon's curse, save avoids).

Equipment: leather armor, cutlass, heavy crossbow, rum, tobacco, and gold trinkets (10 gp total).

Note: The pirates are infected with the demonic plague and are immune to *fear*, *sleep*, and *charm person*. The pirates rise as **zombies** 1d4 rounds after death.

Zombie Pirates (12): HD 2; AC 8[11]; Atk cutlass (1d6) or bite (1d2 + infection); **Move** 6; **Save** 16; **AL** N; **CL/XP** 2/30; **Special:** immune to *sleep* and *charm*, infection (Dagon's curse, save avoids).

Harbor Chain: If engaged, the harbor chain blocks access to the Blood Lagoon and brings any ship to a complete stop. If the ship is moving at a high rate of speed, it suffers structural damage to its keel that requires a minimum of 1d4 days of repairs. The winch for the harbor chain is located in the northern tower.

3. The Lagoon

This inland lagoon is 60 feet deep and has space to hold three sailing ships on its docks. The lagoon serves as a place for seagoing vessels to turn around after being outfitted, and for getting their cargo changed and papers forged.

Docks: Currently, two ships are docked in the lagoon. These are the *War Pig*, and the *Murder Fin*.

War Pig: This 110-foot-long carrack is outfitted with four ballista or cannon to each side in a purpose-built weapons deck below the top deck, as well as a long nine in the fore of the ship. The ship is crewed by a small crew of 34 pirates, though it has enough room to house twice as many men and 80 tons of cargo. Currently, the crew of the *War Pig* is ashore, leaving only **1d4 pirates** on deck to serve as guards, though the ship is quickly crewed and underway if the lagoon is attacked.

The pirates aboard the *War Pig* are infected with the demonic scourge. Despite the ship's armaments, the crew chooses to close with enemies to cut them to pieces and infect survivors with their unholy plague.

Pirates, Male or Female Human Sailors (Ftr1) (1d4): HP 1d8; AC 7[12]; Atk cutlass (1d6), light crossbow (1d4+1) or bite (1d2 + infection); **Move** 12; **Save** 14; **AL** C; **CL/XP** 1/15; **Special:** +2 to hit, infection (Dagon's curse, save avoids).

Equipment: leather armor, cutlass, light crossbow with 10 bolts, rum, tobacco, and gold trinkets (3 gp total).

Note: The pirates are infected with the demonic plague and are immune to *fear*, *sleep*, and *charm person*. The pirates rise as **zombies** 1d4 rounds after death.

Zombie Pirates (varies): HD 2; AC 8[11]; Atk cutlass (1d6) or bite (1d2 + infection); **Move** 6; **Save** 16; **AL** N; **CL/XP** 2/30; **Special:** immune to *sleep* and *charm*, infection (Dagon's curse, save avoids).

Murder Fin: This 80-foot-long caravel carries a crew complement of 20. Fast and light, the *Murder Fin* is outfitted with a ballista (or cannon) at its fore and aft, each swivel mounted and ready to quickly engage enemy vessels. The crew are infected with the demonic plague and are typically ashore or in the jungle spaced out of their mind on hallucinatory fruits and demonic visions. Aboard the ship are **5 zombies**. These pirates died but remain hosts to the demonic possession. These zombies' bites have a chance of infecting their foe with Dagon's plague.

Zombie Pirates (5): HD 2; HP 14, 12x2, 11, 9; AC 8[11]; Atk cutlass (1d6) or bite (1d2 + infection); **Move** 6; **Save** 16; **AL** N; **CL/XP** 2/30; **Special:** immune to *sleep* and *charm*, infection (Dagon's curse, save avoids).

4. Outfitters

This building near the docks serves as an outfitters and lumberyard to service and repair pirate ships that put into port at the Blood Lagoon.

Faynor and his servants ran the operation before the arrival of Merevok upon the unwitting pirate colony. Faynor remains in his shop, but he is in a decidedly different form than before, completely dominated by the demon essence. His servants also transformed and now hunger for the flesh and souls of those unfortunates possessed of a living soul that cross their path.

Faynor (Wight): HD 3; HP 19; AC 5[14]; Atk claw (1 + level drain); **Move** 9; **Save** 14; **AL** C; **CL/XP** 6/400; **Special:** +1 magical or silver weapon to hit, level drain (1 level per hit).

Faynor's Servants (Ghouls) (5): HD 2; HP 15, 13, 12, 10x2; AC 6[13]; Atk 2 claws (1d3 + paralysis), bite (1d4); **Move** 9; **Save** 16; **AL** C; **CL/XP** 3/60; **Special:** immunities (*charm*, *sleep*), paralyzing touch (3d6 turns, save avoids).

Faynor and his ghouls attack anyone who enters the establishment.

If the curse is somehow lifted, Faynor and his servants fall down dead and immediately begin to decompose. However, a *raise dead* spell could revive them.

Treasure: There are 1,000 pounds of hard tack, 1,000 pounds of sugar, four kegs of rum, 1,000 feet of rope, a set of spare sails, a spare, anchor, a ton of raw lumber, two barrels of nails, and 10 barrels of pitch here, as well as a full complement of woodworking tools.

5. Jail

This masonry and palm thatch building housed the Blood Lagoon traders' headquarters. The pirates use it as a jail for captured hostages they ransom away to other ports, and as holding cells for captives taken as booty during their pirate raids.

When Merevok came down from the mountain, he freed all of the captives and demanded that they accept Dagon as their lord in exchange for their freedom. Many did, while others fled into the jungle.

Currently, four hostages are in the cells, though they starved to death and rose as **4 ghouls**.

Ghouls (4): HD 2; HP 14, 13, 11, 10; AC 6[13]; Atk 2 claws (1d3 + paralysis), bite (1d4); **Move** 9; **Save** 16; **AL** C; **CL/XP** 3/60; **Special:** immunities (*charm*, *sleep*), paralyzing touch (3d6 turns, save avoids).

The overseers' office holds documents indicating trade with the Northman Jarl Harlan Narwal and Bulut Zultar of the Cloud Oasis.

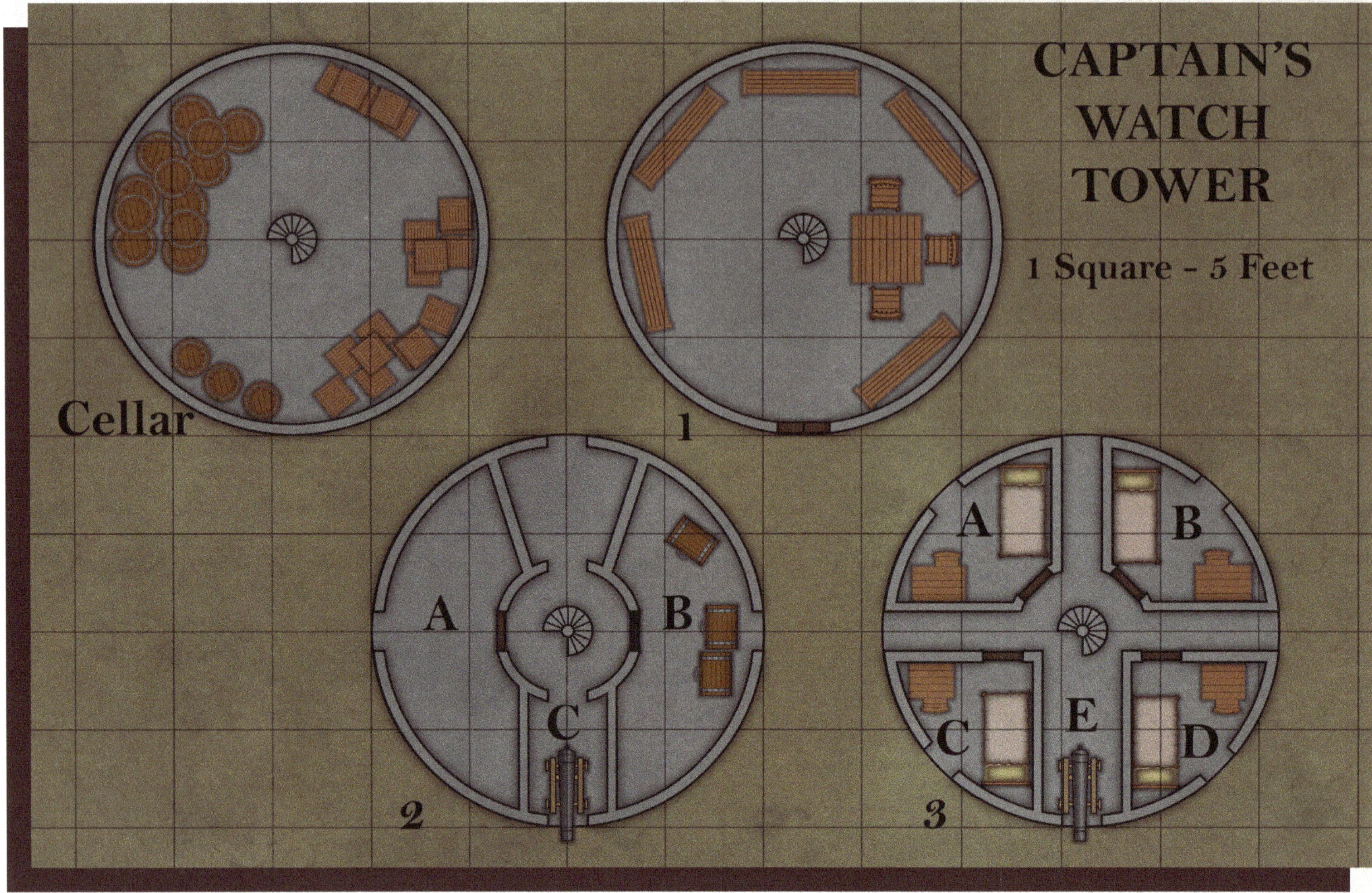

6. Captain's Watchtower

This 50-foot-tall cement block and seashell watchtower commands a strong view of the lagoon harbor. The tower once housed Lord Stanwyck's captain of the guard. The lower rooms were used to house stores of dried goods and a quartermaster who managed the equipment used by Stanwyck's guards. It now serves as the stronghold and de-facto bank for the pirates' collective treasury.

Standard Features

Concrete: The tower is made from concrete formed from native sand, seashells, and lime from lime pits on the interior of the island.

Spiral Stair: A spiral stair runs through the center of the tower and leads to each floor and the rooftop. The staircase makes a clockwise turn so that defenders in the upper floors gain a +1 to attacks against invaders from below.

Cellar

The cellar holds dried goods including 100 crates of hard tack, 20 barrels of salted pork, 20 barrels of pickled fish, 20 barrels of salted fish, 20 barrels of rum, 10 barrels of pickled eggs, and 30 kegs of pale ale. Each barrel or crate of rations is equal to four weeks of food for 10 men.

The cellar has become home to **4 giant centipedes**.

Giant Centipede (7ft) (4): HD 2; **HP** 15, 13, 12, 9; **AC** 5[14]; **Atk** bite (1d8 + poison); **Move** 15; **Save** 16; **AL** N; **CL/XP** 3/60; **Special:** poison bite (+6 save or die).

Ground Floor

The entry doors to the tower are bronze bound and made from tropical hardwood. They are bound from the inside and require a *knock* spell, battering ram, or some other mighty physical means to overcome. The lower floor is a circular room with a table and chairs in its center. The walls are adorned with weapon racks holding 10 heavy crossbows, 10 light crossbows, 10 cutlasses, 10 heavy maces, and six heavily oiled suits of chainmail.

There are **5 guards** on the ground floor. Each is afflicted with the demonic curse, which causes them to fly into a fit of rage and attack any non-infected. They fight to the death.

Guards, Male or Female Humans (5): HD 1; **HP** 8, 6x2, 5, 4; **AC** 7[12]; **Atk** cutlass (1d6) or bite (1d2 + infection); **Move** 12; **Save** 17; **AL** L; **CL/XP** 1/15; **Special:** +2 to hit, infection (Dagon's curse, save avoids).

Equipment: leather armor, longsword.

Note: The guards are infected with the demonic plague and are immune to *fear, sleep,* and *charm person*. The guards rise as **zombies** 1d4 rounds after death.

Zombie Pirates (varies): HD 2; **AC** 8[11]; **Atk** cutlass (1d6) or bite (1d2 + infection); **Move** 6; **Save** 16; **AL** N; **CL/XP** 2/30; **Special:** immune to *sleep* and *charm*, infection (Dagon's curse, save avoids).

Second Floor

The second floor houses the quartermaster for what once served as the mercantile exchange before the coming of Merevok. Mr. Slim, the quartermaster, was a shrewd accountant and an accomplished forger before the demonic spirits possessed him.

A. Mr. Slim's Room: Mr. Slim swore his oath to Dagon when Merevok arrived wielding his magic scroll, and he quickly succumbed to the influence of the dark lord of the seas. Now Mr. Slim spends his days calculating how best to spread the demonic infection across the lands. These unending numbers cover the walls, floor, ceiling, desk, and every scrap of parchment in his chambers. Bits of string hang from pins, attached to wall maps and globes. Opened volumes of books reference the customs and locations of the various kingdoms within sailing distance of the Blood Lagoon.

If the curse is somehow removed, Mr. Slim returns to his normal, somewhat less nefarious form.

BLOOD LAGOON
1 Square – 100 Yards
N
1
2
3
4
5
6
7
8
9
10
11
12
13
14
15

Mr. Slim, Male Human Quartermaster (Thf6): HP 19; AC 6[13]; **Atk** *+1 rapier* (1d6+1) or bite (1d2 + infection); **Move** 12; **Save** 10; **AL** C; **CL/XP** 6/400; **Special:** +2 save bonus vs. traps and magical devices, +2 to hit, backstab (x3), infection (Dagon's curse, save avoids), read languages, thieving skills.

Thieving Skills: Climb 90%, Tasks/Traps 40%, Hear 4 in 6, Hide 35%, Silent 45%, Locks 35%.

Equipment: *+1 leather armor, +1 rapier, boots of elvenkind,* satchel containing 30 gp, sapphire worth 200 gp, golden bracelet (20 gp) and gold rope chain (200 gp).

Note: Mr. Slim is infected with the demonic plague and is immune to *fear, sleep,* and *charm person.* He rises as a **hungry zombie** 1d4 rounds after death.

Hungry Zombie: HD 2; HP 13; AC 8 [11]; **Atk** strike (1d6 + grab and bite + infection), weapon (1d8); **Move** 6; **Save** 16; **AL** N; **CL/XP** 3/60; **Special:** grab and bite (automatic 1d4 damage after strike), infection (Dagon's curse, save avoids). (*Tome of Horrors 4* 243)

B. Safe Room: A stout, locked iron door serves as the vault for the pirate treasury. The lock is a set combination known only to Mr. Slim, though most ships' captains know at least one of the numbers in the combination so that any three of them together may open the vault in the event of the untimely demise of Mr. Slim.

Due to Mr. Slim's transformation, he is unfortunately not in the position to share his knowledge with others. The lock itself is magical in nature and is 90% resistant to a *knock* spell, though *dispel magic* (vs. an 11th-level magic-user) could be used to remove this penalty for 1d6 rounds.

Failing to pick the lock (–10% penalty to the attempt) triggers a **poison gas trap** that fills the hallway with noxious fumes that require characters to make a saving throw or suffer 2d6 points of poison damage per round. The gas dissipates in 1d4 + 2 rounds.

Inside the safe room is 1,000 pounds of gold melted into flat one-pound ingots valued at 10 gp each. There is also 2,000 pounds of silver melted into flat one-pound ingots worth 1 gp each.

While within the treasure room, the treasure cannot be touched by anyone not bearing the chain tattoo of the master or the skull tattoo of the Brotherhood of Skulls. Doing otherwise summons an **efreeti** to the chamber. The efreeti sets upon thieves with great vigor.

Nocan Demir (Efreeti): HD 10; HP 68; AC 2[17]; **Atk** fist or sword (1d8+5); **Move** 9 (fly 24); **Save** 5; **AL** C; **CL/XP** 12/2000; **Special:** wall of fire (as spell).

C. The Long Gun: The pirates installed a nine-pound cannon in the window here after they took control of the lagoon. The cannon affords sweeping protection for the pirates over their new holding. It did not, however, protect them from Merevok. Under normal circumstances the pirates have a good idea when ships enter the river, and the cannon is crewed and ready to fire.

Third Floor: Captains' Quarters

Four lushly adorned apartments on the third floor serve as land-based quarters for visiting ships' captains. The quartermaster rents them for 10 gp per week during standard months.

A. Captain Greox's Quarters: Captain **Greox** is a hobgoblin captain of the *War Pig.* Greox succumbed to the power of the demonic worms, as has his crew. He has a 50% chance of being in his quarters; otherwise, he can be found at the Tin Cup Inn (**Area 9**) or aboard his ship.

Scars crisscross Greox's arms, hands, thighs, and face from countless battles at close quarters. He is an able fighter and rules his crew of half orcs, hobgoblins, and men with an iron claw. Like his crew, Greox is currently possessed by the demonic plague and is compelled to spread the curse to others. If the curse is removed, Greox returns to his normal, albeit equally terrible state of rotten, bloodthirsty evil.

Captain Greox, Male Hobgoblin Sailor (Ftr7): HP 51; AC 3[16]; **Atk** *+1 cutlass* (1d6+7), *+1 handaxe*

(1d6+7), heavy crossbow (1d6+2, *+1 bolt*) or bite (1d2 + infection); **Move** 12; **Save** 6 (+2, ring); **AL** C; **CL/XP** 7/600; **Special:** +2 to hit, infection (Dagon's curse, save avoids), multiple attacks (7) vs. creatures with 1 or fewer HD.

Equipment: *gauntlets of ogre power, +1 cutlass, +1 handaxe,* heavy crossbow and 20 *+1 bolts, ring of protection +2.*

Note: Greox is infected with the demonic plague and is immune to *fear, sleep,* and *charm person.* He rises as a **brain-eating zombie** 1d4 rounds after death.

Brain-eating Zombie: HD 3; HP 19; AC 8[11]; **Atk** strike (1d8) or bite (1d2 + infection); **Move** 6; **Save** 14; **AL** C; **CL/XP** 5/240; **Special:** absorbs spells (up to 2d4 levels of spells), infection (Dagon's curse, save avoids). (*Monstrosities* 530)

Greox attacks intruders with the ruthlessness of a jungle cat, the plague driving him to battle past his own senses and sense of survival. He attempts to bite and infect whomever he can with Dagon's curse. The majority of his crew billets in abandoned cottages along the shore, with his executive staff keeping rooms at the Tin Cup Inn.

Treasure: Greox, despite his outward gruffness and foul stench, is a creature who enjoys the comforts of silk, velvet, and fine furs. His wardrobe is filled with expensive fabrics, corsets, vests, and silk dresses stolen from ships he has raided or from the wardrobe of Lady Marie Stanwyck that have been re-tailored to his unique size and shape. The clothing is worth 2,000 gp and would fill a steamer chest. He also keeps 500 gp in gold coins, 1,000 sp, a string of white pearls worth 200 gp, and four pairs of gold and diamond earrings worth 40 gp each.

B. Captain Shaughnessey's Quarters: Careen Shaughnessey, captain of the *Murder Fin,* keeps these quarters when at port in the Blood Lagoon. A former mate of Captain Bethany, Careen has succumbed to the demonic essence and is soon to depart at the behest of Dagon to spread the plague to civilized lands.

Careen's crew is composed of mostly female pirates of a variety of races and skills. They, too, are filled with the essence of the demonic curse and currently keep their barracks in the old barracks house in **Area 7**. In the room, Careen has a bed, dresser, and makeup table that weigh more than 1,000 pounds and have a value of 2,500 gp. These once belonged to Lady Marie Stanwyck and were brought to Careen's chambers when Lord Stanwyck was captured and his house sacked.

Captain Careen Saughnessey, Female Human Sailor (Clr4/Thf2): HP 25; AC 4[15]; **Atk** *+1 mace* (1d6+1) or bite (1d2 + infection); **Move** 12 (30ft leap); **Save** 11 (+1, ring); **AL** C; **CL/XP** 6/400; **Special:** +2 save versus paralysis and poison, +2 save bonus vs. traps and magical devices, +2 to hit, backstab (x2), control undead, infection (Dagon's curse, save avoids), spells (2/1), read languages, thieving skills.

Spells: 1st—*cause light wounds* (x2); 2nd—*silence 15ft radius.*

Thieving Skills: Climb 86%, Tasks/Traps 20%, Hear 3 in 6, Hide 15%, Silent 25%, Locks 15%;

Equipment: chainmail, *+1 mace, boots of leaping, ring of protection +1.*

Note: Careen is infected with the demonic plague and is immune to *fear, sleep,* and *charm person.* She rises as a **brine zombie** 1d4 rounds after death.

Brine Zombie Careen: HD 4; HP 25; AC 5[14]; **Atk** *+1 mace* (1d6+1 + 1d6 poison) or bite (1d2 + infection); **Move** 12 (swim 12); **Save** 12 (+1, ring); **AL** C; **CL/XP** 4/120; **Special:** immune to *sleep* and *charm,* infection (Dagon's curse, save avoids), resistance to fire (50%), *ring of protection +1.* (*The Tome of Horrors Complete* 614)

Treasure: Careen has a locked silver coffer in the floorboards of her room that is trapped with a **poison dart trap**. The trap fires four darts outward in a fan shape. Each dart attacks a random character within 20 feet as a 3HD creature and is tipped with a poison that does 2d6 points of damage (save for half).

Within the chest are 100 pp, a sack full of 10 rubies worth 500 gp each, a silver dagger with a jeweled handle worth 60 gp, a *wand of invisibility* (5 charges), a *scroll of raise dead,* three *scrolls of cure serious wounds,* a *scroll of bless,* two *potions of healing*, and a scroll indicating the Underguild as the true identity of Duloth's benefactors. (For more about the Underguild, see *Sewers of the Underguild* in **Quests of Doom** by **Frog God Games**.)

C. Empty Quarters: These chambers are reserved for any captain of the Brotherhood of Skulls who comes into port at the Blood Lagoon. The room is adorned with a four-poster bed set with mosquito netting, a dresser, cupboard, side table, desk, and ironbound locking chest with an excellent lock. As only two vessels are currently in the harbor, the chamber is unoccupied.

D. Red-Handed Jaquez Quarters: These quarters are currently empty save for a hidden treasure map tucked under the mattress that Jaquez misplaced. The map shows the location of the Isle of Bonjo Tombo and a drawing of the Wheel of Chaos.

E. Long Gun: This cannon is exactly like the one located on the second floor. It does, however, have a hairline crack on the underside of its brass body that has not been noticed. The next time this cannon is fired, it has a 50% chance of exploding.

Roof

The roof of the tower serves as a lookout post. A huge bronze and glass brazier sits atop the tower. Lifting a metal shield from the glass reveals an ever-burning flame inside a refracting device designed to cast light into the harbor after dark to allow navigation of the lagoon when necessary. The brazier is shielded to prevent light from leaking out and confusing the pirates.

Two lookouts are selected from crews docked within the lagoon and ordered to keep the watch in four-hour shifts. The **2 guards** stationed here currently are infected with Dagon's curse and seek mainly to infect others — forgetting to sound the alarm that intruders are occupying the parapet.

Long Gun: A long gun here is identical to the ones on the floors below. When the pirates are of sound mind, they have the guns prepared to fire on any enemy that would enter the lagoon, right at the point where a ship would be hung up on the Blood Lagoon's chains (**Area 2**).

Guards, Male or Female Humans (2): HD 1; HP 6, 5; AC 7[12]; **Atk** cutlass (1d6) or bite (1d2 + infection); **Move** 12; **Save** 17; **AL** L; **CL/ XP** 1/15; **Special**: +2 to hit, infection (Dagon's curse, save avoids). **Equipment**: leather armor, longsword.

Note: The guards are infected with the demonic plague and are immune to *fear*, *sleep*, and *charm person*. The guards rise as **zombies** 1d4 rounds after death.

Zombie Pirates (varies): HD 2; AC 8[11]; Atk cutlass (1d6) or bite (1d2 + infection); **Move** 6; **Save** 16; **AL** N; **CL/XP** 2/30; **Special:** immune to *sleep* and *charm*, infection (Dagon's curse, save avoids).

7. Guard Barracks

This building served as the guard barracks for Lord Stanwyck's troops. It now serves as a flophouse of sorts for crewmen who do not wish to sleep aboard ship. Currently, the crewmen from the *Murder Fin* are billeted here as they busy themselves preparing for an expedition to spread Dagon's plague across the shipping lanes.

***Murder Fin* Marines, Male or Female Humans (Ftr1) (5):** HP 8, 7, 6x2, 5; AC 7[12]; **Atk** cutlass (1d6), light crossbow (1d4+1) or bite (1d2 + infection); **Move** 12; **Save** 14; **AL** C; **CL/XP** 1/15; **Special**: +2 to hit, infection (Dagon's curse, save avoids).

Equipment: leather armor, cutlass, light crossbow with 20 bolts, 1d10 gp.

Note: The marines are infected with the demonic plague and are immune to *fear*, *sleep*, and *charm person*. They rise as **zombies** 1d4 rounds after death.

***Murder Fin* Pirates, Male or Female Humans (Thf1) (5):** HP 4x2, 3, 2x2; AC 7[12]; **Atk** rapier (1d6), dagger (1d4), light crossbow (1d4+1) or bite (1d2 + infection); **Move** 12; **Save** 15; **AL** C; **CL/ XP** 1/15; **Special**: +2 save bonus vs. traps and magical devices, +2 to hit, backstab (x2), infection (Dagon's curse, save avoids), read languages, thieving skills.

Thieving Skills: Climb 85%, Tasks/Traps 15%, Hear 3 in 6, Hide 10%, Silent 20%, Locks 10%;

Equipment: leather armor, rapier, dagger, light crossbow with 20 bolts, 1d10 gp.

Note: The pirates are infected with the demonic plague and are immune to *fear*, *sleep*, and *charm person*. The pirates rise as **zombies** 1d4 rounds after death.

Zombie Pirates (varies): HD 2; AC 8[11]; Atk cutlass (1d6) or bite (1d2 + infection); **Move** 6; **Save** 16; **AL** N; **CL/XP** 2/30; **Special:** immune to *sleep* and *charm*, infection (Dagon's curse, save avoids).

8. Shrine of Dagon

This temple recently was converted to the worship of Dagon, and the idols of the other gods were smashed at the foot of a nine-foot-tall painted wooden fetish of the Deep One. The fetish appears in the form of a demonic human torso carved from native wood. Its lower half appears to have been made from a crudely taxidermied fish of great size. A human skull wearing a beaten gold crown is mounted for a head.

The shrine emanates an aura of evil that is palpable to paladins, clerics or those using *detect evil*. Indeed, the shrine imposes a –1 penalty to hit and saves on Lawful characters. The evil aura can be removed by dousing the shrine in holy water and casting *bless*.

However, attempting to cleanse the shrine has a 50% chance of summoning a **hydrodaemon** to protect the idol.

Hydrodaemon: HD 7; **HP** 43; **AC** 0[19]; **Atk** 2 claws (1d6), bite (2d6) or spit (sleep); **Move** 9 (swim 24, fly 12); **Save** 9; **AL** C; **CL/ XP** 13/2300; **Special: immunities** +1 magical or silver weapon to hit, (acid, poison), magic resistance (35%), spells, spittle (20ft, save or sleep for 6 rounds), summon elemental (1/day, water elemental), telepathy (100ft). (***The Tome of Horrors Complete*** 120)

Spells: at will—*darkness 15ft radius*, *detect magic*, *dimension door*, *fear*.

The crown is from an ancient civilization of sea people whose lands were drowned by the ocean more than a thousand years ago. It is otherwise worthless except as a historical relic. The wood forming the idol's torso comes from an upland tree found in the island's interior at a higher elevation than the lower wetlands where the lagoon is located.

Destroying the shrine allows all characters and pirates within 500 feet to make a saving throw to shake off the effects of Dagon's curse. This includes any pirates in **Areas 6**, **7**, and **9**.

A careful search of the shrine uncovers a secret panel within the torso of the idol that holds the following clerical scrolls: *cure serious wounds* (x3), *hold person*, *restoration*, *raise dead*, *speak with the dead* (x2), and *water breathing*.

Note: Pirates freed of the curse are not necessarily any friendlier to the characters if encountered. They are, after all, pirates, and the characters are still intruders in their secret lair. Allow characters to negotiate with any of the pirates, assuming that the pirates are still ready for a fight and largely ungrateful for their rescue.

9. Tin Cup Inn

The Tin Cup Inn is a two-story, 12-room inn serving as a watering hole and gathering space for travelers going back to the time when Lord Stanwyck ruled the lagoon. The inn contains a common room, kitchen, Tim and Sarah's room, a storeroom, and eight private rooms on the second story capable of sleeping 2–4 guests each.

Sweet Sarah (N female human waitress, 9 hp) and **Big Tim** (N male human bartender, 15 hp) run the Tin Cup Inn. A large, badly dented tin cup the size of a bucket hangs outside its swinging doors. A dozen pirates in various states of rum-addled stupors litter the common room. Under normal circumstances, Tim stands behind the bar with a bloodstained, ash-handled paddle to keep the greasy fingers of wanton sailors away from Sarah, who serves drinks and sharp comments to patrons.

Tim and Sarah have been careful not to actually kill any of the crew of the *War Pig* who have been using their inn as a flophouse while awaiting orders for their mission to infect shipping to the mainland as they don't want to have any issues with any of the ships' captains who frequent the Blood Lagoon.

The couple barricaded themselves in the back. With access to the dried goods, a kitchen, and their private quarters, they are not starving, though they are harried and weary from frequent attempts to capture them and infect them with the curse. Sarah and Tim are torn, because they were friends with many of the pirates occupying the Blood Lagoon, and are horrified by the change in them.

A few months ago, Merevok arrived from the interior of the island and walked into the pirate enclosure accompanied by a band of pirates acting oddly. These pirates were the crew of the *War Pig* who frequently hunted in the jungle interior for wild boar and "magic fruit" they ate for its narcotic effects.

Merevok met with the captains of the *Murder Fin*, *War Pig*, and *The Golden Snake*, and somehow convinced the trio to follow him into the jungle. The captains then returned and led their ships' officers into the jungle. A day later, members of the crew began their trek upriver to the island's central mountain.

Before long, those who returned began acting erratically, attacking, and biting their shipmates in a bizarre fashion considered brutal even by the standards of pirates.

Sarah and Tim speak of tiny wriggling worms they have seen in the mouths and at the back of the throats of the pirates. A strange gurgling also comes from their mouths of the pirates when they speak. Since their encounters with Merevok, the normally rum-thirsty pirates have eschewed any alcohol.

A total of **12 pirates** are spread throughout the inn. The pirates at the inn are mostly humans.

Pirates, Male or Female Human Sailors (Ftr1) (12): HP 8, 7x2, 6x4, 5x2, 4x3; AC 7[12]; **Atk** cutlass (1d6), light crossbow (1d4+1) or bite (1d2 + infection); **Move** 12; **Save** 14; **AL** C; **CL/XP** 1/15; **Special:** +2 to hit, infection (Dagon's curse, save avoids).

Equipment: leather armor, cutlass, light crossbow with 10 bolts, rum, tobacco, and gold trinkets (3 gp total).

Note: The pirates are infected with the demonic plague and are immune to *fear*, *sleep*, and *charm person*. The pirates rise as **zombies** 1d4 rounds after death.

Zombie Pirates (varies): HD 2; AC 8[11]; **Atk** cutlass (1d6) or bite (1d2 + infection); **Move** 6; **Save** 16; **AL** N; **CL/XP** 2/30; **Special:** immune to *sleep* and *charm*, infection (Dagon's curse, save avoids).

10. Shoreside Cottages

The shore-side cottages each hold **1d4 + 2 pirates** from the crew of the *War Pig*. They are either orcs or hobgoblins infected with the curse of Dagon. They appear to be busying themselves for a sea voyage. The beasts have 1d4 gp each.

Pirates, Male or Female Human Sailors (Ftr1) (1d4 + 2): HP 1d8; AC 7[12]; **Atk** cutlass (1d6), light crossbow (1d4+1) or bite (1d2 + infection); **Move** 12; **Save** 14; **AL** C; **CL/XP** 1/15; **Special:** +2 to hit, infection (Dagon's curse, save avoids).

Equipment: leather armor, cutlass, light crossbow with 10 bolts, rum, tobacco, and gold trinkets (1d4 gp total).

Note: The pirates are infected with the demonic plague and are immune to *fear*, *sleep*, and *charm person*. The pirates rise as **zombies** 1d4 rounds after death.

Zombie Pirates (varies): HD 2; AC 8[11]; **Atk** cutlass (1d6) or bite (1d2 + infection); **Move** 6; **Save** 16; **AL** N; **CL/XP** 2/30; **Special:** immune to *sleep* and *charm*, infection (Dagon's curse, save avoids).

11. Estate Gate

The gates are currently closed. Vines cover them in a thick, twining mass, effectively locking the gate. The palisade wall around the estate is 10 feet high and made of sharpened tree trunks coated in creosote and sunk six feet into the ground. Despite this, they are an easy climb for anyone with a climb ability or those carrying a rope and grapple.

12. Fields

The fields contain overgrown sugar cane and groves of bananas that have not been picked in months. The overgrown nature makes the area as thick as any jungle, forming an almost impenetrable barrier. Moving through the banana and cane requires hacking a path that reduces movement by two-thirds and quickly causes fatigue in the tropical/subtropical heat.

Dangerous creatures that crept onto the estate's grounds after the upheaval wrought by Merevok's arrival now dwell in the overgrown fields.

1d12	Encounter
1	1d6 pirate ghouls
2	1d3 bloody bones
3	Giant crocodile
4	2d6 giant rats
5–12	No encounter

Giant Crocodile: This encounter is with a **giant crocodile**. It attacks anything the size of a skiff or smaller, looking to capsize the vessel and drown anyone thrown into the water for later consumption.

Giant Crocodile: HD 6; AC 3[16]; **Atk** bite (3d6), tail (1d6); **Move** 9 (swim 12); **Save** 11; **AL** N; **CL/XP** 6/400; **Special:** none. (*Monstrosities* 78)

Bloody Bones: This is an encounter with a gang of former overseers butchered by their captives as they made their way to freedom during the chaos of Merevok's arrival. The **1d3 bloody bones** attempt to capture anyone they encounter with the shackles of death.

Bloody Bones (1d3): HD 5; AC 3[16]; **Atk** 2 claws (1d6), 4 tendrils (hold); **Move** 12; **Save** 12; **AL** C; **CL/XP** 7/600; **Special:** resist fire (50%), slippery, tendrils (save or be held, 10hp, AC 3[16]). (*The Tome of Horrors Complete* 63)

Giant Rats: This is an encounter with **2d6 giant rats** who have set up a nest among the sugar cane.

Giant Rats (2d6): HD 1d4hp; AC 7[12]; **Atk** bite (1d3); **Move** 12; **Save** 18; **AL** N; **CL/XP** A/5; **Special:** 5% are diseased.

Pirate Ghouls: These **1d6 ghouls**, dressed in the trappings of the pirates of the Blood Lagoon, wander the island in search of rotted flesh to eat. They are infected with Dagon's curse.

Pirate Ghouls (1d6): HD 2; AC 6[13]; **Atk** 2 claws (1d3 + paralysis), bite (1d4 + infection); **Move** 9; **Save** 16; **AL** C; **CL/XP** 3/60; **Special:** +2 to hit, immunities (*charm*, *sleep*), infection (Dagon's curse, save avoids), paralyzing touch (3d6 turns, save avoids).

Note: The ghouls are infected with Dagon's curse. They rise as **zombies** 1d4 rounds after death.

Zombies (varies): HD 2; AC 8[11]; **Atk** cutlass (1d6) or bite (1d2 + infection); **Move** 6; **Save** 16; **AL** N; **CL/XP** 2/30; **Special:** immune to *sleep* and *charm*, infection (Dagon's curse, save avoids).

13. Rum Distillery

Buried in a tall mass of trees is the shack used by Lord Stanwyck's master distiller to brew the rich brown blackstrap rum that he traded throughout the region. Three dozen barrels contain 53 gallons of rum each. Twelve of these barrels are five years old, 12 are 10 years old, and another 12 are raw rum. The rums here are over 50% alcohol and highly flammable. The rum manufacturing ended roughly around the time of the arrival of Merevok, who has yet to burn the distillery to the ground as he is unaware of the curse's weakness to the strong spirit.

Spencer O'Joy, Lord Stanwyck's distiller and rum taster, is hiding from the cursed and the dead in the rafters of the warehouse next to the still. If the characters search the rafters, they find Spencer cowering in a corner with a bottle of rum.

Spencer's rum has a unique power over the demonic worms that infect the pirates of the Blood Lagoon, and cures the curse immediately. Spencer blesses every cask of rum in the name of Bacchus Dionysus.

Spencer O'Joy, Male Human Distiller (Clr6): HP 25; AC 5[14]; **Atk** mace (1d6); **Move** 12; **Save** 10; **AL** N; **CL/XP** 6/400; **Special:** +2 save vs. paralysis and poison, turn undead, spells (2/2/1/1).

Spells: 1st—*cure light wounds*, *purify food and drink*; 2nd—*bless* (x2); 3rd—*cure disease*; 4th—*cure serious wounds*.

Equipment: chainmail, mace, *ring of invisibility*.

Spencer has been the master distiller since Lord Stanwyck brought him here. The pirates spared him due to the quality of his rum. Living on the southern end of the lagoon, he was far enough away from the madness of Merevok's arrival, and has thus far gone unnoticed as he hides from wandering ghouls and marauding pirates infected with Dagon's curse. Spencer is not much of a combatant and avoids conflict as best he can.

If the characters discover the power of his rum, he gladly offers them as much of the stuff as they can carry. If the characters free him from the island, he offers to work off the cost of his passage by providing his services as a master distiller.

14. Captives' Quarters

These quarters show the signs of a massacre. The cruel overseers were butchered here before rising as undead monstrosities.

The quarters are made up of a long low house filled with 18 doublewide bunks. The large central barracks is flanked on each side by guard bunkhouses and equipment chambers filled with shackles and implements of torture designed to keep the servants in line and wary at all times.

14-1. Overseer's Quarters

This was the quarters of Karnelious Brogue, Lord Stanwyck's overseer. Karnelious was particularly cruel and met a fate similar to his master. Through the power of Dagon's curse, Karnelious rose as a **rawbones** and now patrols the halls, his bloody whip in his hand.

His room contains a stained mattress, an iron holy symbol of the master, and a pair of broken shackles. The room is otherwise empty of treasure of any value.

Karnelious Brogue (Rawbones): HD 8; **HP** 56; **AC** 4[15]; **Atk** 2 slams (1d8) or entrail lash (1d4 + strangulation); **Move** 6; **Save** 8; **AL** C; **CL/XP** 10/1400; **Special:** +1 or better magical weapons to hit, immune to cold, nauseating aura (20ft radius, −1 to hit and saves, save avoids), strangulation (save or entangled, automatic 1d4 damage until freed), vomit gore (3/day, 20ft cone, 6d6 damage, save for half). (***The Tome of Horrors Complete*** 456)

Karnelious attacks with his horrible stench, vomiting gore on foes and moaning commands to his bloody bones to capture the characters and "teach them a lesson."

14-2. Western Guard Room

This room once served as a bunkhouse for overseers who served under Karnelious. They were murdered when Merevok freed the servants, but have risen from death as **4 bloody bones**. Like Karnelious' room, this room is empty of any valuables.

Bloody Bones (4): HD 5; **HP** 34, 30, 29, 27; **AC** 3[16]; **Atk** 2 claws (1d6), 4 tendrils (hold); **Move** 12; **Save** 12; **AL** C; **CL/XP** 7/600; **Special:** resist fire (50%), slippery, tendrils (save or be held, 10hp, AC 3[16]). (***The Tome of Horrors Complete*** 63)

14-3. Eastern Guard Room

This room is identical to the **Western Guard Room (Area 14-2)**.

Bloody Bones (4): HD 5; **HP** 37, 32, 30, 24; **AC** 3[16]; **Atk** 2 claws (1d6), 4 tendrils (hold); **Move** 12; **Save** 12; **AL** C; **CL/XP** 7/600; **Special:** resist fire (50%), slippery, tendrils (save or be held, 10hp, AC 3[16]). (***The Tome of Horrors Complete*** 63)

14-4. Irons and Chains

This room holds irons and manacles. A shrine to the master stands in one corner and features his bald visage staring down from an idol carved from jet worth 200 gp. The entire chamber emanates an aura of evil that makes those who enter feel hopeless and uncomfortable until they leave the room. Within this room are 10 bullwhips, 100 pairs of manacles, bolts, 200 feet of chain, and 200 feet of hemp rope.

14-5. Captives' Quarters

This large dormitory once housed nearly 100 captives who slept two or more to a bunk or on the floor on woven mats. The room is patrolled by **4 bloody bones** who look to chain anyone they find.

Bloody Bones (4): HD 5; **HP** 33, 31, 26, 23; **AC** 3[16]; **Atk** 2 claws (1d6), 4 tendrils (hold); **Move** 12; **Save** 12; **AL** C; **CL/XP** 7/600; **Special:** resist fire (50%), slippery, tendrils (save or be held, 10hp, AC 3[16]). (***The Tome of Horrors Complete*** 63)

14-6. Gallows

The desiccated corpse of Lord Stanwyck hangs from the gallows where he once hung escaped captives as a warning to others. Lord Stanwyck's corpse has turned a putrid shade of purple due to the jungle-like heat.

Stanwyck's body is dressed in his sleeping finery, though it is threadbare and rotted. A closer examination of his corpse reveals a space where a signet ring once sat upon his finger, but is now missing. The ring would serve as "proof of death" for any assassination contract or royal inquest. Currently, Merevok possesses the ring.

If characters approach the body, it opens its eyes, revealing a horrific visage that quickly fades. This is Lord Stanwyck's ghost. Characters must make a successful save or flee in terror (as a *fear* spell). Characters who flee must make a saving throw afterward or be unwilling to return to the presence of the gallows, and cannot be made to do so under any circumstances. They are also now more susceptible to possession by Stanwyck's spirit (−4 on saves against being possessed by the evil spirit in the future).

14-7. Equipment Shed

The equipment shed is where all machetes, cane knives, hoes, scythes, and other equipment were stored. The lock is broken off. Remaining in the equipment shed are seven machetes, a scythe, and two cane knives, as well as six pairs of chaps that protect against rattlesnake bites.

Lord Stanwyck's Estate: The Great House

This two-story wood and stucco home and its cursed grounds occupy the southern shores of the lagoon.

The whitewashed estate house now has black mold growing over it from disuse. Storm shutters are nailed shut over all the windows. Its doors are broken and remain open from the riot that took place as the servants dragged their former master from his bed, beat him, and hung him in an orgy of blood and revenge.

Stanwyck's home is haunted by a lifetime of horrors he wrought during his reign over the island, culminating in the cursed spirit of **Lord Stanwyck's ghost**.

Stanwyck's Ghost: The ghost of Lord Vayne Stanwyck haunts the grounds of his estate, though it is at its strongest inside the home itself. The ghost may be encountered in any of the estate's rooms. It attempts to separate the group either through strange noises or by scaring them into splitting up. Any character seeing his ghost's frightening visage must make a saving throw or run in fear in a random direction for 1d6 rounds. Once characters separate, Stanwyck's ghost pursues a solo target and attempts to possess the character in an attempt to lead the party to Merevok's lair inside the mountain. Anyone he attempts to possess must make a saving throw to throw off the effect. If the ghost has already scared a character within the past 24 hours, the save is made with a –4 penalty. Trigger manifestations are detailed in several of the rooms that may be used by Stanwyck's ghost. The Referee may select the best manifestation for the party or roll randomly to determine where Stanwyck's ghost appears. Referees can also create their own manifestations to increase the horror quotient of the haunted house.

If Stanwyck's ghost is turned, his spirit flees for as long as is necessary before returning to haunt the party. The ghost avoids physical combat with the characters until it possesses a character and convinces the party to go to the mountain in the center of the island.

Lord Vayne Stanwyck (Ghost): HD 5; HP 38; AC 0[19]; **Atk** strangulation (save or die in 1d4+1 rounds); **Move** 12 (fly); **Save** 12; **AL** C; **CL/XP** 7/600; **Special:** +1 magical or silver weapon to hit, frightful presence (as *fear* spell, save resists), magic resistance (50%), possess (save avoids, –4 if previously frightened by ghost), strangles (if hit, save or die in 1d4+1 rounds).

Note: Lord Stanwyck desires to possess a character to carry him to the mountain in the center of the island. Failing that, he attempts to kill the intruders to his home.

If at any time Stanwyck's ghost possesses a character, the player must be notified either by secret note or through a private conference. The player should still play his or her character normally — with one exception. The character has a strong vision and compulsion of the island's central mountain. They "know" without a doubt that the source of the curse is located there. They "know" that they must make their way to the mountain, immediately, and without any further dalliance. They "know" this because the clues all suddenly clicked in their head. If you have a player who is willing to help you set the hook and sell the possession to the other players, all the better! If not, sweeten the deal with an offer of extra experience points for each person at the table that the player can convince to follow his character to the mountain.

1. Grand Hall

The grand hall of the manor extends from the first to the second story of the house. It is decorated with now-moldering oil paintings of Lord Stanwyck, his wife Marie, his young children, and a painting of his family's ancestral home in the coastal estates to the south of Freegate. A pair of staircases flank the southern wall of the grand hall and lead up to the second story. Double doors flank the hall.

Trigger Manifestation: As the characters explore, Stanwyck's ghost uses its telekinetic powers to slam shut the entrance doors to the north and south of the hall while simultaneously opening the side doors and revealing itself via the portrait of Lord Stanwyck.

Stanwyck uses his frightful presence and the door trick to terrify the party. Characters who flee do so in random directions. The incorporeal and invisible spirit pursues those who end up in one of the hallways.

2. Dining Room

This is where Stanwyck, his late wife Marie, and his children, Vayne III and Georgia, took their dinners before the pirate invasion. The fine china and silverware are long gone, appropriated by the pirates when they looted the lagoon. All that remains is a large, luxuriant table and chairs made of padauk wood that weighs several hundred pounds. The table and chairs are worth 2,000 gp regionally, but likely worth three times that amount in farther coastal regions. The dried, rotted remains of a roast boar sit in the center of the table.

Trigger Manifestation: As the characters examine the room, the bones and skull of the boar grow bits of rotted flesh and crawl with flies that quickly swarm the room, taking the form of a human. The horrific sight is Lord Stanwyck's attempt to instill fear in the characters. If a character is already frightened or enters the chamber alone, Stanwyck attempts the use his possession ability to take control of the character.

3. Kitchen

The kitchen is in total disarray. The pantry doors are torn open, and any food that was here is long gone. All that remains is a thick patch of **memory moss** that grew under the larder.

Memory Moss: When a living creature moves within 60 feet of a patch of memory moss, it attacks by attempting to steal that creature's memories. It can target a single creature each round. A targeted creature must succeed on a saving throw or lose all memories from the last 24 hours. This is particularly nasty to spellcasters, who lose all spells prepared within the last 24 hours. Once a memory moss steals a creature's memories, it sinks back down and does not attack again for one day. Any creature who loses its memories to the memory moss acts as if affected by a *confusion* spell for the next 1d4 hours. Lost memories can be regained by eating the memory moss that absorbed them. Doing so requires a saving throw, with failure resulting in the creature being nauseated for 1d6 minutes and suffering 2d4 points of damage. (***The Tome of Horrors Complete*** 377)

The moss attempts to snatch memories from the characters as they explore the kitchen. The moss was small before the coming of Merevok. Eating the moss gives characters insight into the pirate raid on the Blood Lagoon and Stanwyck's subsequent imprisonment in his own home. Roll 1d6 or select a memory from the table below:

1d6	Memory
1	**Pirate Attack:** Servants working in the kitchen are terrified as they hear the roar of cannon. They flee out the back.
2	**Stanwyck's Missing Children:** Stanwyck's children vanished before the pirate assault. This caused great strife between Stanwyck and Lady Marie, and weakened Stanwyck's forces on the island as he lost dozens of his best soldiers trying to find the missing children.
3–4	**Stanwyck's Hanging:** Stanwyck's fear and anger are palpable, and fill the mind of the eater as he is hauled out of the manor and hanged by an angry mob. A robed figure stands at the gates to the estate watching with a cruel smile on his lips.
5	**Stanwyck's Family Secrets:** A servant tells a much younger Lord Stanwyck that Sessenni is raising Stanwyck's illegitimate child. Fearing for herself and the life of her son, Sessenni fled and was captured, but the boy fell into the river and is assumed to have drowned. Stanwyck is angered at the runaway, angered at the thought of the child he fathered with Sessenni, and also its loss. This anger is mixed with terror that his wife might find out about the bastard.
6	**Marie Stanwyck:** This is a memory from Vayne Stanwyck's wife. She found out about Lord Stanwyck's illegitimate child and sent Karnelious Brogue to kill Sessenni and her 10-year-old son.

A staircase in the southern corner of the kitchen leads to **The Cellar (Area 12)**.

4. Study

This room served as Lord Stanwyck's study. The pirates largely pilfered the room, scouring through his documents for maps, passwords, lock combinations, and legal papers. The drawers of the once-fine burled mahogany desk are pulled free, and it has been tipped onto its side to reveal a once-hidden compartment. A portrait of Lord Stanwyck with his two young children and a faithful hunting dog is hidden beneath a shawl in one corner of the room.

Trigger Manifestation: If the shawl is removed, the painting seems to come to life, with the faces of the children becoming pale and drawn, eventually decomposing, as the face of their father turns purple. The dog takes on a hellish visage.

5. The Butler's Quarters

The room is neat and tidy, having a single bed, a dresser, nightstand, and desk. Lying on the floor, his back to the wall, is a drawn and pale corpse. Its mouth hangs open in an expression of terror, and its throat has been crushed. The body looks to be that of someone who is easily more than 100 years old, though his attire looks neatly pressed and well cared for. If the corpse is touched, it literally crumbles to dust.

This was the private quarters of Geal, Lord Stanwyck's butler. Geal managed the house and the estate as surely as his master did. Geal's diary tells pieces of the family's secrets.

Diary

Geals diary notes his knowledge of the master's infidelity with Sessenni. Characters gain more insight in Lord Stanwyck and his family's secrets determined by the length of time they spend reading the diary.

15 Minutes Reading: Geal's diary tells how Lord Stanwyck strangled his wife after their children went missing. Geal heard a struggle in the mistress's room and loud voices arguing the day before she was found hanging in her chambers. Geal is uncertain — but knows well Lord Stanwyck's temper.

30 Minutes Reading: Geal is grateful he was allowed to remain with Lord Stanwyck during his confinement to the estate. Geal further fears that once ransomed to family on the mainland, he will be traded to the captains or killed for their pleasure.

45 Minutes Reading: Geal describes chaos at the pirate camp and an uprising among the servants. Geal hid as Lord Stanwyck was dragged into the yard, beaten, and hanged. Several servants looked for Geal as well, but he knew the estate well enough to observe without being seen. Geal describes a cruel-faced young man in wizard's robes observing Lord Stanwyck's hanging, and how the man's face bore a familiarity that chilled him to his very core.

1 Hour Reading: Geal's last entry in his diary describes having the sensation that although he is alone in the great house, something is in the house with him. There are noises in the mistress's chambers, and he has smelled the tobacco that Lord Stanwyck liked to smoke on more than one occasion.

If the characters attempt to contact Geal via *speak with the dead* or a similar spell, they find that the last thing he saw as he hid in the manor house was the apparition of Lord Stanwyck. This spirit embraced him and drained the life from his bones. **Trigger Manifestation:** There is a chance that the ghost of Lord Stanwyck animates the corpse and uses his frightful presence ability to terrify the characters. If a character explores Geal's room alone, Stanwyck attempts to possess the character.

6. Maids' Quarters

This room has three beds. Clothes in the dresser look like the clothes worn by a maid or servant. The room is otherwise ransacked of valuables.

7. Marie's Room

This door has been nailed shut with silver nails from the outside, and a *protection from evil 10ft radius* spell has been cast upon the space before door. The sound of a woman's crying is heard clearly through the door. The weeping is palpable, as is the sobbing hatred in the woman's voice. This was the room of Lady Marie, who is now a **grey spirit** haunting her former home. Marie attacks anyone who enters the room, screaming how their failure has cost them her children!

Marie the Grey Spirit: HD 6; HP 32; AC 2[17]; Atk touch (2d6 + level drain); **Move** 12 (fly); **Save** 11; **AL** C; **CL/ XP** 12/2000; **Special:** +1 or better magical or silver weapons to hit, frightful presence (30ft radius, save or stunned for 2d6 rounds, see **Ravages of Death's Gaze** below), harbinger (tragedy occurs within 1d6 days), incorporeal, ravages of death gaze, rejuvenation (2d4 days after death). (*Tome of Horrors 4* 114)

This room was stripped almost bare, though markings on the floor indicate where a fine bed, dresser, and makeup table once stood. Careen Shaughnessey claimed these items as booty.

A door to the south is boarded and nailed shut. It requires an Open Doors check (with a −2 penalty) to break this door open immediately, or a crowbar and several minutes to pry the boards free. The doorway leads to Lord Stanwyck's bedroom.

Ravages of Death's Gaze: The horror of Marie's last days are visited upon characters who fail their save when first looking upon the spirit. They are first filled with a joyous hope as they sense the wonders of a young woman sent in marriage by her noble family to her betrothed upon a beautiful tropical isle. Her joy is enhanced as she gives birth to her new husband's twins nine months later. The visions turn darker after the twins are born as she notices a servant woman giving her foul looks and intent on cursing the young bride and mother with the evil eye. The woman seems to always be accompanied by a youthful boy who carries the familiar look of her husband upon his face. The visions turn to darkness and melancholy as she discovers the truth of the boy's parentage and that her husband still offers his favors to the boy's mother. The visions turn to fury, followed by fear and horror as the couple fight over the disappearance of their own children, culminating in Marie's strangulation at the hands of her wrathful husband.

8. Lord Stanwyck's Room

The door to this room was once locked, but the lock is broken and lies on the floor. Inside the room is a fine bed that has been torn to shreds, with its silk draperies shredded, and the goose down mattress cut open so that feathers cover the floor. The shutters are closed, and the room is exceptionally dark. The dresser drawers are torn open, and the furniture has been overturned. A sense of despair and palpable darkness fills the room.

If turned previously, Lord Stanwyck's ghost is in the chamber where he spent his last few months alive and imprisoned by the pirates. Stanwyck materializes only if forced to do so, and otherwise attempts to possess a character if he is able.

Confronting Stanwyck with his sins only angers him further. His spirit has an uncomfortable existence with the spirit of his wife, whom he avoids at all cost. Getting the two spirits in the same area causes them to argue with one another about his failings and infidelity, though neither can physically hurt the other.

If not turned, Stanwyck is in this room only if a character comes into the chamber alone. He then appears to possess the character.

9. Nursery

The Stanwyck children used this chamber as a playroom. There are various children's books filled with nursery rhymes, including one book attributed to the "Mathen Twins," which is filled with creepy tales of children feeding their friends to monsters, told in the manner of nursery rhymes and children's singalong songs. The book is worth 200 gp to a library or collector.

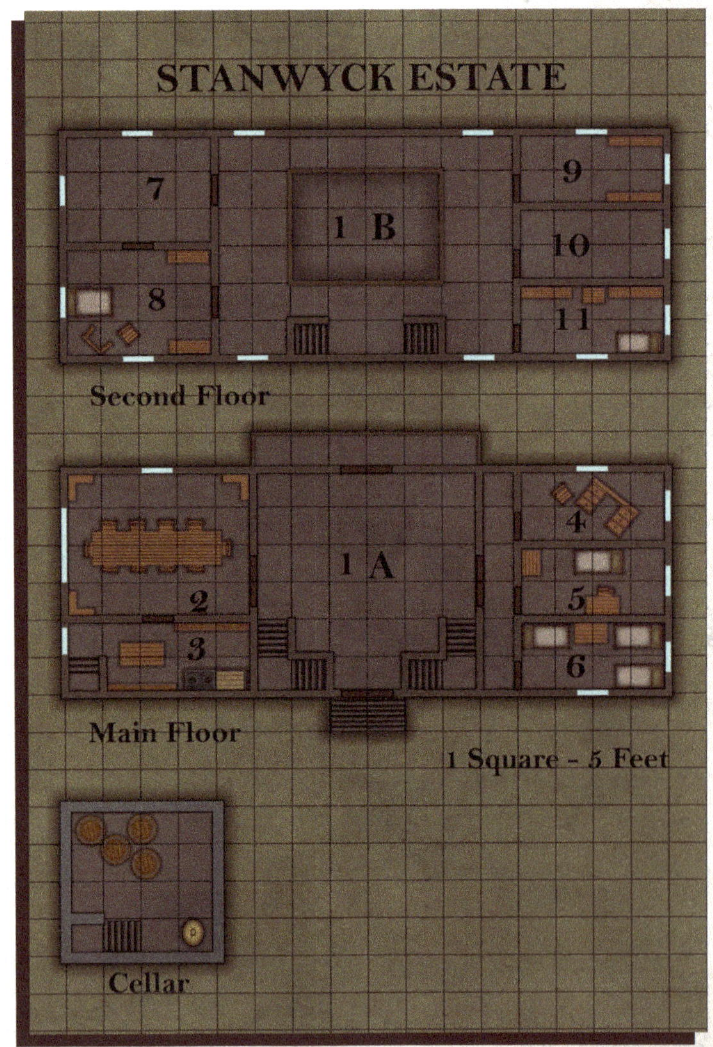

Among the other items are toys built by Carlo Polindina. The toys seem mildly grotesque, but are of high quality and craftsmanship. The following toys can be found around the room:

The King: This toy is mildly animated, and has black hair and a finely manicured blond goatee and a crown of real gold. When its beard is stroked, the doll exclaims "Hail to the King, Baby." It is worth 200 gp.

The Princess: This toy, similar to the king, is very honest. If touched by someone who is old, it says, "You are old. Let me alone." If touched by someone who is dirty or bloody from fighting, "You're too nasty to play with a princess." It continues with similar insults whenever handled. The doll is worth 200 gp.

The Horse: This toy is a rocking horse built for a small child. The horse rocks itself when the rider exclaims the word "gallop." It stops when the word "whoa" is spoken. The horse can count to 10 by dipping its mane and swishing its tail if told to "count." The rocking horse is worth 300 gp.

Huntsman: This doll is grotesque, having a bulbous nose and bushy black beard. He has a real bow and arrows, and a real hatchet. If told to "track," the doll takes off and tracks like a real ranger, returning after one day with the directions to the location of whoever it was told to track. If told to "hunt," the huntsman goes out and attempts to kill any creature smaller than itself. The huntsman brings back a small dog, cat, squirrel, or birds up to the size of a large crow. Typically, the children ordered it to hunt rats. The huntsman is a miniature **clockwork warrior** that is following its programming to be a child's toy (and sometimes more):

Clockwork Warrior: HD 2; **HP** 12; **AC** 5[14]; **Atk** hand axe (1d3); **Move** 9; **Save** 16; **AL** N; **CL/ XP** 3/60; **Special:** self-repair (1hp/round). (*Tome of Horrors 4* 114)

10. Vayne III's Room

This was the room of Lord Stanwyck's 8-year-old son. The room has been ransacked like the other rooms in the estate, and little remains here to pick through that has any value. A scribble on a piece of parchment shows a charcoal drawing of a stick figure boy and girl standing with a tall stick figure man in a fancy hat.

Trigger Manifestation: Whoever is holding the drawing is fascinated as suddenly the figures begin to move. The "father figure" becomes strikingly realistic and reaches out from the drawing to clutch at the face of the viewer, forcing the character to make a saving throw or be possessed.

11. Georgia's Room

This child's room is untouched, and its door is locked tightly. For whatever reason, this room avoided being sacked along with the estate. Within the room is a four-poster bed fitted with a mosquito net and silk sheets worth 200 gp. A wardrobe is filled with tiny silk and satin dresses, and several pairs of shoes and bonnets that match each dress. The clothes are worth about 1,500 gp.

Trigger Manifestation: As soon as anyone turns their back, a wisp of air blows past their ear and they turn to see a dress, with bonnet, parasol, and shoes standing behind them. This manifestation steps toward them …

12. The Cellar

Beneath the kitchen is a storage cellar where dried goods were kept. Most of the food has been raided from the kitchen, as have the dried fruits, and Lord Stanwyck's collection of wine. What remains untouched are four 40-gallon kegs of rum, and six cured hams, and a 20-pound sack of fried banana chips.

Merevok's Mountain

This mountain rises from the high rainforest in the central highland of the island. Merevok's mountain is an extinct volcano that serves as Merevok's fortress and base of operations. The Vayne River passes the foot of the mountain at a close juncture.

1. Up the River

Boat passage becomes impossible as the characters reach the foot of the mountain and the river turns into a series of waterfalls fed by natural springs and runoff from the rainforest. Ancient ladder-like handholds are carved into the stonework, built alongside these waterfalls and rock walls, leading to the Grotto of Dagon. These are not a difficult climb under normal circumstances. Unfortunately for the characters, islanders and former captives loyal to Merevok take aim at anyone attempting entry into Merevok's lair without the explicit invitation of the wizard himself.

2. The Islanders are Restless

Islanders and freed captives who joined Merevok's cause dwell along the banks of the river in the high mountain forest. Bodies of pirates who strayed too far without Merevok's permission are impaled along the trail. Their bodies show signs of torture. The servants are mostly timid, as they have seen the depredations of pirates eating the crazy fruit, and the horrific visage of those who come out of Merevok's lair.

Islanders (Ftr1) (2d10): HD 1d8; **AC** 9[10]; **Atk** spear (1d6); **Move** 12; **Save** 14; **AL** N; **CL/XP** 1/15; **Special:** rage (+1 to hit and damage, 4 rounds/day).
Equipment: spear.
A bamboo and rope bridge beyond the camp leads to the Grotto of Dagon.

3. The Cavern Entrance

A **pair of Merevok's chosen guards** watch this entrance.
Guards (Ftr4) (2): HP 31, 29; **AC** 7[12]; **Atk** stone hand axe (1d8+1); **Move** 12; **Save** 11; **AL** C; **CL/XP** 4/120; **Special:** multiple attacks (4) vs. creatures with 1 or fewer HD, +1 to hit and damage, rage (+1 to hit and damage, 8 rounds/day).
Equipment: leather armor, stone hand axe.

4. The Grotto of Dagon

This large cave stands next to the extinct core of the volcanic mountain. The cenote formed here is filled with seawater and spring water fed from hundreds of ancient lava tubes far below the mountain. An obsidian statue of Dagon stands in the northeast corner of the cavern, its sinuous tail sunk into the waters with its torso exposed above the waterline. One hand reaches up to grasp at the ceiling of the chamber while the other holds a thick scale the size of a tower shield half in and half out of the water.

The 30-foot-tall statue emanates a powerful aura of evil and forces any Lawful beings to make a saving throw or suffer a –2 to all saves, attack rolls, and damage for the duration of their time within this ancient temple. The scale held in the stony claw of the statue wriggles with millions of thin, pointed, red-and-black worms that make the brackish water of the cenote boil with an unholy life.

The Waters: The waters crawl with the worms of Dagon. Anyone touching the water must make a saving throw or be infected with the curse of Dagon. A bridge from the western side of the grotto leads to a platform that stands before the *scale of Dagon*.

Merevok holds council in the grotto with his sea brides as they pray and work rituals to further the power of the Demon of the Deep.

Brides of Merevok (Dagon-Blessed Sahuagin) (4): HD 4+1; **HP** 30, 29x2, 27; **AC** 5[14]; **Atk** coral-edged club (1d6+2, 1d6+4 vs. Lawful); **Move** 12 (swim 18); **Save** 13; **AL** C; **CL/XP** 5/240; **Special:** +2 to hit and damage vs. Lawful creatures. (*Monstrosities* 407)
Merevok (Ftr4/MU7): HP 45; **AC** 3[16] or 2[17] (missile) from *shield* spell; **Atk** *staff of striking* (2d6); **Move** 12; **Save** 8 (+1, ring); **AL** C; **CL/XP** 12/2000; **Special:** spells (4/3/2/1).
Spells: 1st—*magic missile* (x2), *protection from good, shield*; 2nd—*invisibility, mirror image, web*; 3rd—*dispel magic, lightning bolt*;

4th—*dimension door*.

Equipment: *bracers of defense AC 4[15], ring of protection +1, staff of striking, wand of lightning* (4 charges)

Merevok was a 10-year-old boy when the jealous Lady Marie sent Karnelious Brogue to kill him and his mother. Sessenni was caught and tortured to death, but Merevok fell into the Vayne River and was presumed lost. He survived in the hills for days before stumbling upon the Grotto of Dagon and giving himself to the watery lord. When he finally came of age, he led a small band of possessed pirates against the estate of his estranged father. He converted more pirates to his cause using the worm-filled waters brought forth by the *scale of Dagon* until eventually he was marching at the head of an army of possessed killers. While the Stanwyck family estate and the pirates occupying the lagoon bore the brunt of his initial assault, he has since made plans to spread the curse of Dagon to farther coasts.

A Father and Son Confrontation

If the ghost of Lord Vayne Stanwyck possesses any character, the spirit suddenly leaps forth from the mouth of the character to attack Merevok with its ghostly embrace. The ghost of Lord Stanwyck fights until destroyed, or until Merevok is killed, and then turns on the characters using any abilities in its repertoire to get the characters to destroy the remaining pirates on its behalf.

If Merevok is aware that the characters are approaching, he casts *shield*, *protection from good*, and *mirror image* on himself.

If the characters manage to raid the grotto with pure stealth, then Merevok is unprepared for an attack and uses *protection from good* and *mirror image* as quickly as possible, allowing his brides to soak up any attacks that the characters have to offer.

SCALE OF DAGON

The *scale of Dagon* is a piece of the demon lord Dagon's hide inscribed with unholy script. Worshippers collected these unholy words, and high priests of his sect now covet them. When read aloud and submerged in a pool of water, the scale opens a minor rift to Dagon's aquatic realms of the Abyss and attracts a host of demonic worms to pollute the waters. These unholy nematodes seek to possess and ultimately consume mortal souls for the glory of the watery lord.

The *scale of Dagon* can also serve a secondary purpose to create a nigh-unstoppable dreadnaught to sail the seas. The scale is one of the pieces of the *Ship of Chaos*, and when combined with other items known as the *demon keel*, the *wheel of chaos*, and the *sails of sorrow*, it creates a dreadnaught of incredible power and despicable evil.

Destruction: The scale can be destroyed in an other-planar place of power. For example, it could be smashed on the shadow forge in the Plane of Shadow, melted in the fires of Hell, or crushed under one of the seven gates of Heaven. Casting it into the River Styx immediately returns it to the possession of Dagon.

COMPLETING THE ADVENTURE

Characters can complete the adventure in a variety of ways, though all culminate in removing the *scale of Dagon* and purifying the waters of the grotto. The purification can be accomplished by pouring either 100 gallons of pure holy water into the grotto, or with 20 gallons of blessed rum. Either solution instantly destroys the demonic nematodes.

Characters may then return to their homeland, defeat the now-cured pirates, or conquer the Blood Lagoon for use as a base of operations as they see fit. Ultimately, other adventures may arise due to their dealings in the Blood Lagoon, not the least of which include treasure maps to new and unexplored locations. Some possible continuations of the adventure includes run-ins with the Brotherhood of Skulls or the pursuit of the slaving operation of which Lord Stanwyck's operation was only a small piece.

BROTHERHOOD OF SKULLS

The Brotherhood of Skulls is a loose pirate confederation with allied chapters sailing across all of the known seas. Among its notable sea lords were Cho Sun, captain of the *Rapier*, Bloody Bethany, captain of the *Banshee*, and Duncan Crow, captain of the *Firewitch*, as well as the captains based in the Blood Lagoon.

Before Cho Sun's claim to the title of Sea King, he served under the cruel tutelage of Captain Kang. Kang was a true believer in the seafarers' myth of a *Ship of Chaos* designed for the terrestrial servants of Dagon to wreak havoc on the land walkers. The original ship was destroyed in an epic battle, and its parts were scattered to the seven seas. Kang spent years collecting the pieces of the ship, and was close to completing his task when his allies, fearing his powers, turned on him and again scattered the pieces to the corners of the Lost Lands.

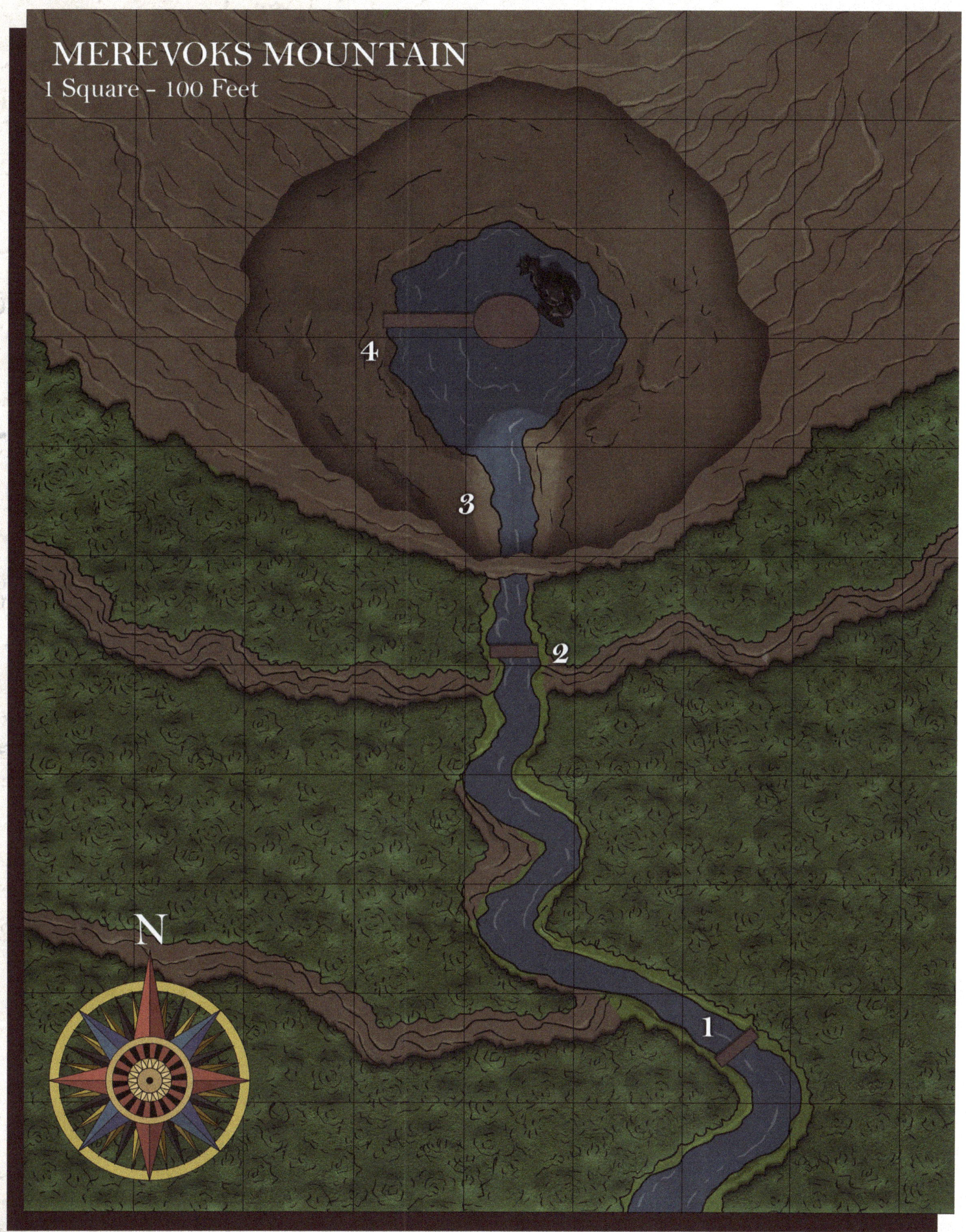

MEREVOKS MOUNTAIN
1 Square - 100 Feet
N
4
3
2
1